The Bishop's Prison

Book 1

Barabbas

By

K. Scott Brown

Hedgewood Press

Based loosely on the wonderful folklore from the *Isle of Man*, this book is not meant to be taken too literally, for I have taken many liberties with the facts. I meant no disrespect for the existing folklore, and it was for literary and creative purposes that I made any alterations. But in truth, I may have made some of these changes out of ignorance, for the existing history is quite large and sometimes open to interpretation. Much of the folklore in this book is purely fictional, having been invented by myself to enhance the existing folklore, and it was my intent to fuse the two together.

The elements dealing with the Bishop and with background of Christianity I have taken from the beautiful and wonderful hagiographies of the Middle Ages. In truth, the hagiographies read very much like some of the Classic Fantasy I loved to read when I was a young man. The real beauty for me came from the mixture of intense faith, with the supernatural aspect of the miracles of the saints. One does not have to believe in the veracity of these miracles for the beauty and wonder to fill one with deep pleasure. And as our own world turns and burns with political and religious turmoil, it is good to step aside occasionally to enjoy a time when faith was a foremost duty in the lives of most men and women hoping to reach heaven.

Throughout the hagiographical literature, it was given to the saints the ability to perform miracles, and just as Christ had brought the dead back to life again, so too did the saints. The saints walked on water, called the dead back to life, exorcised evil spirits, walked through walls, transformed into birds, and other impossible miracles. How so could this be, when the Lord had forbidden sorcery of any kind? But it was not the will of the saints to use the power of the Lord. Rather, it was the power of the Lord to work through the saints. We find it hard to find our own purpose; how much more difficult to understand the purpose of the Lord?

Lastly, in keeping with the structure of *King Bartholomew*, this book is a book of stories, and a book about stories. Our life is a story though we do not know how it will end, and sometimes we even get a chance to speak. Stories speak, stories are alive; they change and grow over time. Sometimes these stories have something to teach, and sometimes the stories change and teach nothing. Children understand stories, and so we must learn to become children again for stories to teach us anything at all and not to become dead and obsolete. Stories with something to teach are called revelations. Stories that are base and teach nothing are called nightmares.

K Scott Brown

June 4, 2017

Table of Contents

Prologue

"The magic is not in the story," said King Sigmus to Iona one morning as they sat together listening to the song of a thrush that was dancing on the pavement at their feet, eating seeds. "The magic is not old. No, the magic is in the mind, and it is the story that allows it to become manifest. In truth Iona, the magic is in your beautiful mind."

"Then why do we continue to remember stories?" Iona replied innocently and the King could see that she was smiling. "Why don't you just make them up?" she insisted.

"Oh, Iona you are so wise in your innocence," the King said with a smile, "for in truth, that is exactly what I do."

Beltane, *the fire of Bel*, is an ancient and still important holiday on the Isle of Man, and so it was during the reign of King Sigmus. In days now long past, bonfires were lit to celebrate the arrival of summer and rebirth. Traditionally on this day house fires were extinguished and then re-lit from hilltop fires honoring fertility gods of old; new fires were lit from the bonfire, flame of Tara, to signify rebirth and there was much dancing. This was also the time midpoint between Spring Equinox and Summer Solstice where the veil between the worlds is thin, allowing fairies and other supernatural beings to crossover. Much mischief was done and many marriages were followed thus.

And so it was that during the week of Beltane King Sigmus opened his own castle grounds for the celebration, but he was not celebrating the ancient rituals of the fertility god, but instead the resurrection of the Lord. For the pagan influences were slowly being replaced with new traditions issued by the Church, and the *Green Man* and *Cernunnos* the horned god were spoken about and remembered in the folklore of the isle, but the people and that they be drawn to Christ still remembered the old ways, for the old ways were part of the island in the trees and the sacred wells and the very soil, and even their dreams were constructed from such powerful pagan mythology.

Everyone knew that King Sigmus had the most wonderful garden and some rumors said that it was an enchanted garden. In truth, the enchantment was not great enough to prevent the tragic and untimely death of Queen Kathryn and their stillborn child who was baptized Bartholomew. After several years of grieving King Sigmus decided to open his fantastic garden once a year to the good people of Man and that they should enjoy all the solace and wonder of such a created thing. The first time, however, that he saw a young boy running through the hedges he was so overcome with grief that he returned to his high tower and stayed away all afternoon. Afterward he would only say that he was tired and allowed himself a rare afternoon nap.

On this day it was his beautiful mistress Iona and not the King that sat in the garden along with a group of children, laughing, playing, and telling stories. The children, who were all dressed in bright colors, wanted to hear about all the legends surrounding the garden. They had all heard the tales from their parents: tales of magical beings, creatures, angels, devils and unicorns. Iona knew them all. Some of the children even believed that the garden was alive and that the dense labyrinthine garden walls opened to vistas of green pastures beyond this world where Pan ran over lush hills piping his lyrical music.

Iona laughed bashfully for she loved the children and couldn't resist teasing them. "Beyond this world, you say? Is this world not enchanted enough for you?" she asked. "When I was a child I chased unicorns across the fields until they would disappear in the twilight."

The children all began to laugh and their eyes sparkled.

"You are right," Iona spoke up suddenly. "The garden is enchanted for even now you are all part of the enchantment. It is said that bad children become lost within the maze and are gone forever. But you are not bad children so follow me to the center and let us see if there be something there for us."

The children clapped their hands together and followed Iona. They all loved Iona, and to them she was a queen, and it was only the adults that remained silent when the name of Iona was mentioned. With a gentle laugh Iona twined her hands together behind her back and skipped into the interior of the hedge-maze like a beautiful sorceress with the children following close behind.

Iona skipped through the narrow pathway between the high hedges for she knew the way and did not become confused by the expertly crafted and convoluted maze. The hedge was so dense that it was impossible to see through it and the children were all amazed by the clever twists and turns that Iona navigated so carelessly. In a few minutes they emerged into the center of the maze which was circular and had a fountain around which many variegated plants and flowers grew. Stone benches on two sides of the fountain offered a place to sit and enjoy the comforting isolation of a garden removed from the everyday world that was a world unto itself. On a stone table next to the benches were trays of tea and sweet confections.

"Look at what I found," Iona said turning to the children with a smile on her face. "Now you children help yourself and get comfortable because in all the excitement I forgot to tell you the story of King Orry's Tower."

Soon everyone was ready and they waited patiently for Iona to begin her tale. And when the last little girl was seated with her treats on the flagstones in front of her bench she began her tale.

"There lived a King named King Orry long ago before written word had come to these shores. This was a time of words, a time of scratching on stones and the carving of symbols, and this was a time of deeds done in the name of honor. This was a violent period and the clashing of swords and the raising of pikes dominated the mind of men. King Orry fought hard to defend his land against invaders and many men had died horrible but noble deaths. Then there came a time when King Orry was driven across his land by the army of a sorceress from the north. He was driven all the way to Bishopscourt where he built a stone tower in which to hide, for the sorceress had come for him. The sorceress had come to usurp his power and subjugate his people.

"Driven to the edge of his land the King made his stand, and there he built a tall, square stone tower so that he could see his enemy from the four points of the Earth. But the sorceress would not give up and she sent strong winds from the four corners of the Earth and she sent stinging, sleeting, freezing rain down from above. Then she battered the walls of his tower with vicious biting insects and with crows, but the King would not come out. Next she prepared to storm the tower and raze it to the ground and she brought her army to the foot of the tower.

"The King's most trusted warriors surrounded his tower and were prepared to fight to the death for their King for they were bound by oaths they had taken. Now the sorceress was not afraid of the King's warriors however, but she hoped to take away the King without the need to kill those that she could take on as her own to use for her own purpose, and so she tried to trick them with powerful visions in the air and powerful visions in their mind. The sorceress sent terrible mists, shifting and turning miasmas, the sorceress sent creeping, gnawing beasts and slimy, slippery monsters with long tentacles, but the warriors held fast and did not run away, but they were frightened and they sent a messenger to speak with the King before their strength should fade.

"Inside the tower, in the dim light cast from torches and candles, the King waited and consulted with his astrologer. It was true that they could not withstand a siege and that their supplies of food and water were limited. King Orry sat at a table and looked at a hastily drawn chart and the astrologer stood behind him and pointed to various numbers and lines and spoke softly into his ear. The astrologer continued to tap his finger on a particular symbol, but King Orry would hear none of it and he stood up boldly.

"'We must enlist the power of Christ!' he shouted. Then he sent for his high priest, and with his high priest praying for the intercession from the Lord, the King paced back and forth inside his tower.

"The sorceress continued to plague the tower with wind and rain and thunderbolts from above. King Orry stood in a high tower window and looked out. Then he shook his fist in defiance and he waited for the power of the Lord to save him. Days passed without a sign and the weariness started to bear down upon his men. Finally he could wait no longer.

"Now it was known that King Orry had four daughters. The four daughters of King Orry were the most beautiful women in the land and none could look on their fair countenance and not be moved to tears. After much thought, the King sent his daughters up into the top level of the tower and seated them in the four quadrants where they could easily be seen from below. When the soldiers saw the beauty of these women their hearts were moved and they ached with pain that such beauty should be immured. In their agony the men could not be persuaded to attack the tower and they refused to take up arms. But the sorceress still did not give up her quest, and in her fury, that is when she wrought her most malevolent act of sorcery and thus sealed the fate for the King.

"The sorceress conjured up creeping, clinging vines to scale the walls of the tower. The vines grew and grew, twining around the tower and all the way to the top, clutching with sharp piercing thorns into the stone. And when the vines were coiled and interlaced about the tower the sorceress caused them to twist. Inside the tower could be heard the terrible sounds and for the first time King Orry began to worry.

"The King consulted his astrologer again but the astrologer refused to speak for he was frightened by the power of such sorcery. King Orry pointed to the door and certain death if the sorceress should capture him alive, and that is when the astrologer spoke. No one knows for sure and many stories differ, but some people say that this is when the King enlisted the help of the old gods, even the prince of darkness who is also named Lucifer.

"Outside the tower the vines fell away, and at the base of the tower, turned into serpents. The serpents chased away the army of the sorceress and chased them all the way to the sea. But the sorceress was not defeated and this is when she wrought her most evil spell which has lasted till this very day. The sorceress bound them forever more captured in the tower, and that they should never come out, but were instead condemned to, like the sirens of Odysseus, cry their mournful cries into the farthest reaches of the island thus quartered. The King was thus condemned to live forever, but in spirit and not in body. When the doors were finally broken down by the King's faithful army after the retreat of the sorceress, only five mounds of white ash were ever discovered. For many years afterward it was discovered that strange wailing could be heard in the winds that swept across the island and that a mournful throbbing could often be heard inside the tower."

The children sat with their mouths hanging open. Some of them were frightened and some of them did not realize that the story was over.

"It's just a story," Iona comforted them. "Do not be afraid, children, for stories are good and stories teach us many things."

"Is the King still trapped in the tower?" one of the children asked.

"Well, I suppose he is," Iona replied.

"Was King Sigmus ever trapped in a tower?" another child asked.

Iona smiled and replied, "What do you think?"

Sometimes the mind can be a prison, and though the stone and mortar be made of blood, and though drafts and sweeping winds blow through the abandoned passages, the prison is solid and the prison is defenseless, and though the wind may howl like cursed pleas from the depths of this prison, it is only the sound of our own tearful regret like dripping water against the walls of our own memories locked away beneath, for a man's home is his castle.

Kerron the Blasphemer

King Sigmus and Bishop Jacob entered together the infamous Bishop's Prison. The coldness penetrated to the bone and the King drew his cloak tightly against the bitterness that rose up from the stones like an icy dagger, for the very stones of the infernal prison were forged in the coldness of hell. Together they came and would ascend to the very top of the tower, the highest level where the pariah Barabbas was being incarcerated. Bishop Jacob had come to the prison many times, but the top of the tower where Barabbas was kept was forbidden to anyone but the keeper. The Bishop could never enter the prison without the memories overpowering him, and as he placed his foot on the first step of the long, winding stairwell that would take him to the top, he remembered the first time he had met the prisoner Kerron the Blasphemer, and his heart was troubled.

The stone abutment, merging the horrors of hell and the savage guilt of man, rises from the sea like a mist, solid yet ethereal and vaporous as sin itself. Atop the monolith rests the stone structure, buttressed against the sheer wind and bitterness of cold isolation until the prison over time has been absorbed into the cragged stone like a festering wound. Through the landing, Bishop Jacob held fast to the edge of the boat against the choppy, roiling sea. The dangerous waters near the prison were seldom traversed except for those with business. For days the weather had been stormy and unusually inclement, but he was anxious to make his vigil once again at the prison to listen to the lamentations of those for whom such a place was feared. Storm clouds scudded across the leaden sky and the wind lashed at the Bishop's black cloak. With difficulty the boat landed against an outcrop of rock that jutted out to sea and served as a pier. The boatman shouted through the wind.

"I'll be back before the sun goes down! Be careful now and step lively!"

The Bishop hoisted a small bag onto the rocky surface and then stepped out of the boat nimbly, for he was used to this transit and had lost his fear. Then, with a nod to the boatman, he grabbed the front of the bow and shoved hard. As if on cue the torrid sky opened up and it began to rain. The Bishop hurriedly picked up his bag and shuffled as quickly as possible up the slippery stone steps cut into the rock that led to the only way in or out of the dreaded prison.

The prison, raised upon the freezing rock like a dais, looked lonely and frightening against the dark clouds. Bishop Jacob pounded on the iron door and waited to be admitted by the keeper. He was let in at once, for the keeper had watched his tiny vessel as it approached. The Bishop stepped through the doorway and shivered.

"It is a cold rain Stephan, a cold rain indeed."

"Take off your cloak and have some tea," Stephan answered with a nod. "I have been expecting you for a long time now. It is good to see you again, sir."

"I do not envy you for what you must do Stephan, but you have served the King well by your devotion. This is a forsaken place indeed."

Even with the key-lights taken out it was dreadfully dark inside. Accustomed to such gloominess, Stephan seldom took them out. Jacob waited for his eyes to adjust before looking around the familiar prison for signs of hope, but there is no hope for abandoned men. Built as a tower, the prison pierced the sky like a broken finger. A circular stairwell traversed the outer edge of the tower and rose to the top, where a final cell was occupied by the lowliest, most reprehensible soul ever committed. Impenetrable, impregnable, the tower was feared by all that could see its silhouette against the western sky. The walls were built of stone, the floor was paved with stone, the air itself was cold and petrified by the anguish within, and were it not for the softness of the flesh interred, the prison itself would petrify.

"Follow me," said Stephan, and then he led the way to his tiny office where a pot of water heated on a brazier against the wall. As coal was the only source of heat, a constant odor of burning coal filled the prison like a rising vapor from the underworld, and the prisoners continually choked upon the poisonous fumes for the air was stagnant inside with the stench of hell.

Soon Bishop Jacob was sipping a cup of steaming tea and waiting to hear the latest news from Stephan, the keeper, who suffered along with those in his charge.

"I buried the *wailer* last week. Not another soul witnessed his burial at sea."

"I hope he is at peace now," Jacob said sadly. "He deeply regretted his transgression and pleaded for mercy. I told him that only the Lord could grant such mercy, but he is past mercy now . . ."

"Alas," Stephan muttered softly.

"And what became of the [1]*blasphemer*," Stephan? "Tell me then, is *Kerron the Blasphemer* still here?"

"I'm afraid so," Stephan replied. "The King is none too fond of blasphemy."

"That is true," said Jacob thoughtfully as a memory distracted him briefly. "In truth Stephan, to blaspheme in spirit is no different than to utter blasphemous words, for to the Lord they are equivalent. And to guard our thoughts against such a sin is painful to the Lord. Better not to think at all then to tempt such sin. But what about Himmer, is *Himmer the Village Killer* still alive?"

"The last time I looked in on him he was still alive. But, I confess Jacob that I do not look in on him more often than it is necessary to feed him and bring him a few lumps of coal. Yes, he lives . . . that and no more."

"Does he speak?" Jacob asked, as if to learn as much as he could, or as if to share some of the horror of the forsaken man.

"His lamentations are almost too much for me to bear. I consider myself fortunate if I hear nothing from him at all."

"I should like to see the *blasphemer*," said Bishop Jacob suddenly.

The two men stopped in front of an iron door. The keeper silently slid the door panel aside and peered into the cell. Satisfied with what he saw, he inserted the key into the door and unlocked it. Then he stood aside and waited for the Bishop to enter. Finally he locked the door and went away.

The Bishop stood in the doorway and waited for it to close behind him. When it did he remained motionless and waited for the *blasphemer* to speak.

[2]*Kerron the Blasphemer* lay curled up in a corner. He held close to a soiled blanket for protection against crawling demons and demons of the mind. He looked up when Jacob entered.

"Have you come to kill me?" he asked.

---

[1] But he that shall blaspheme against the Holy Ghost, shall never have forgiveness, but shall be guilty of an everlasting sin. Mark 3:29

[2] King Sigmus knew that to blaspheme one must know and willingly blaspheme against the living spirit of God. He sent Kerron to the Bishop's prison so that his pride would be broken by such loneliness and despair and that he would come to know God, and that because he had not known God when he uttered the blasphemy, he could not truly have been a blasphemer.

Jacob looked at the blasphemer and nodded. "No," he said at last. "I have not come to judge."

"Are you of this world?"

Jacob looked closer at the pathetic man. He lay in the corner and shook with fear. His hair was long and fell about his face in dirty, oily streaks. The chalkiness of his skin and his silent trembling showed that he was already sick, and through his pale eyes he stared at the one that should accuse him, for he was dressed in the garments of the church.

"You have nothing to fear from me," Bishop Jacob said softly. Then the bishop opened his bag and removed something: it was a tomato. Moving closer to the blasphemer he reached out his hand. "Take this and eat it," he said, "for I know that you are hungry."

The blasphemer snatched it away quickly, but he did not eat it. Holding it in his hands he felt its softness against the harshness of his cell. Then he looked up to the Bishop and stared through his weary eyes as if the Bishop were an apparition.

"How long have you been here?" Jacob asked compassionately.

The blasphemer did not answer but only held tighter to the tomato fearing that it would vanish.

"Do you remember your sin, Kerron? Tell me so that I may know of your torment."

Still the blasphemer would not speak. He was utterly frightened and feared to reveal his presence as if the tiny blanket could hide him through the dimness of his isolation.

"Are you a blasphemer, Kerron? Is that why you were sent here? Tell me your story and I will remain silent. It is good to share your pain, Kerron. It is good to . . ."

"Yes," the hollow voice of the blasphemer came at last. "His voice was weak and the dimness of his cell only made it weaker.

The Bishop moved slightly and slowly sat down on the edge of his little pallet. He looked directly at the forsaken man and said.

~ 5 ~

"Go ahead now, Kerron . . . tell me your story."

The blasphemer looked long and hard at the Bishop. At first he was afraid to meet his eyes, but after a few moments he looked into the Bishop's eyes and saw that they were true and there was no mockery in them. His own eyes began to sting with the bitterness of unrequited tears. Then he began to speak.

"Sheep's wool has been my trade for my whole life. It's all I know and all I ever wanted to know. My sheep were mine and I protected them just as a parish priest protects his flock. Many nights I ran out into the storm to find a missing sheep because it was my duty to bring it back into the fold, do you understand? Sometimes the darkness can be frightening, but to the tender heart of a sheep the terrors of the night can destroy just as surely as the fangs of a beast or the quick hands of a thief.

"Me and my family lived in a little stone cottage near the western sea so that we could taste the air of Ireland, the land of the saints, and sometimes we prayed to the saints that they might bring us sunshine and good dreams. But mostly we prayed to the Lord, because we knew that to the Lord it was we that were sheep and we were comforted because we knew that a good shepherd protects his sheep against all matter of evil. The Lord gave me three healthy children and I gave the Lord my soul and the souls of my family. The Lord was happy with my soul I reckoned because he kept me safe.

"Now, as you probably know, there are monsters creeping in the shadows and that they not be seen is due to the grace of God. The Lord wants to protect us because we are weak. It is sometimes that I would hear them and even see shadows, for the shadow cast by a demon can reach into the heart of men. The Lord gave this ability to me because the Lord is also a shepherd and gave me a greater sensitivity to such things as demons and crawling monsters the better for me to protect my flock.

"One night as we were all sleeping, one of the children was frightened by a sound in the night. Children also have the ability to penetrate the curtain that separates the world from that which is hidden. She woke up and could not be calmed down again. She trembled like a lost sheep in a storm. I took little [3]Aalin in my arms and held her until she fell to sleep again. I held her until daybreak. In the morning I went out to check on my flock.

"My sheep are free to wander the rocky hillock amongst the stones and grasses and they are content. Most of what is left of an old stone fence built in the last century is in ruins, but it is enough for my sheep to know their boundaries. In

---

[3] Aalin: beautiful.

truth, I have no need of fences. My worries are not that my sheep should escape, but that something should come in from outside.

"I walked around looking for any sign of intrusion and my flock gathered around me bleating and murmuring as if they were frightened. I talked to them gently and told them that they were safe and that seemed to calm them as the sound of a mother's voice comforts her children.

"That night I sent my two boys out into the night to keep watch until morning, and I slept fitfully. When I woke in the morning I had a queer feeling and I bolted out of the cottage to check on the fold. Both of my boys were gathered around a fallen sheep. They were shaking their heads in confusion as neither one of them had heard anything unordinary during the night, and they feared that I would blame them for falling to sleep. I looked down at the fallen ewe and she was ripped open and her insides were strewn about. The other sheep fidgeted and tried to get closer but I held them back. Looking up at my boys from where I was kneeling beside my sheep, I shot them a questioning glance, for I had no idea what kind of animal could have done such a thing, not a fox, no, certainly not a fox. This was the work of a wolf, a lone wolf I speculated.

"I said nothing to my boys at first. But secretly I was alarmed. I knew that the wound was not the work of a wolf. Indeed, a wolf would have devoured part of the flesh for wolves do not attack without driving hunger. Further, I knew that there were no wolves on the island for they were hunted and killed long ago.

"That night I took watch and sent my young boys to bed. The night air is alive with night sounds and it takes a man many years to distinguish the merely nocturnal from the supernatural. The night sounds tell a story of death and rebirth, but it is not suited for the ears of weak men. Slowly I began to succumb to the power of the night, but just before I went under I heard a murmur in the fold. Suddenly I jumped up alert and ready for a fight, and I drew a long dagger from my belt. Now, though the moon was nigh, thick clouds floated above and only a dim half-light illuminated the hillock where I stood ready to defend my flock. Then I saw a shadow moving across the slope near the stone wall. The shadow was darker than the darkness through which it moved. I lunged! When I caught up to the shadow it was gone and only an icy thickness remained.

"I counted my sheep, and when I was satisfied that they were all accounted for I began to relax and consider other things. The stalking predator was unsuccessful . . . I had prevailed, but for how long? I would continue to keep vigil as long as possible, but would I always prevail? The next morning when the sun was up I knew that my sheep would be safe during the daylight hours, so I had a talk with my two boys. I told them that we were being stalked by a demon and that we would have to fight. Yes, they were frightened, I was frightened too. But I told them that the Lord was on our side, for He was also a shepherd. I said that we were righteous in our cause.

"That day we made preparations for our campaign against the demon. We fashioned weapons out of steel and wood and stone, and we plotted against the demon. Little Aalin we did not tell for I had no desire to frighten her needlessly. But as expected, when she saw that we were fashioning weapons, she became curious and begged to be allowed to help. I told her that she was too young for hunting wolves and that she would be safe in the cottage. 'Close the shutters,' I said. 'And don't look out.'

"For three nights we kept the demon at bay, chasing it away when it came too close to our firelight, praying, always mindful of our sheep. And now it seemed like we were getting the upper hand, driving the demon further and further from our property until it lurked outside of our border like a starving soldier, exiled from his camp . . . and still we remained vigilant.

"During daylight hours we would take turns sleeping. My boys were brave and they were strong, but after a fortnight of battle we were exhausted. And then it happened.

"One night after chasing the demon away once more, we heard a cry in the night. It was the sound of absolute terror and it made my blood curdle. Wailing, relentless wailing, the sound stopped me cold. And then suddenly I recognized that terrible sound . . . it was the voice of Aalin.

"I ran with all the strength of my soul just as the last wail faded into the darkness. I ran with all my strength, at last bursting into my cottage and running to her little room, but when I got there, the shutters were torn open and it looked like a terrible struggle had taken place. Aalin was gone . . . Aalin was taken."

It took a moment for Bishop Jacob to realize that he was finished speaking. There was a terrible silence. In the choking silence the Bishop could feel the pressure of the walls as if his nerves were expanded against the frigid prison walls. Finally Kerron looked up and his eyes met the eyes of the Bishop and the strength of the Bishop failed him for the first time in his life. Overcome by the grief of the harrowing tale, the Bishop wanted nothing more than to comfort the poor man who had lost his child. He looked into the eyes of the prisoner . . . they were blank.

"What kind of a shepherd allows his flock to be taken away from under his very nose?" said Kerron weakly. "What kind of a shepherd?"

"It was not your fault," said Bishop Jacob with compassion, but his words failed him. "It was not your fault," he repeated.

But then the expression of Kerron changed and the change was terrible. He slowly raised his arm and in his hand he still clutched the tomato given to him by Jacob. He was trembling. His awful eyes stabbed into the Bishop mercilessly and in his anger he shouted as his hand crushed the tomato between his fingers.

"I was not talking about myself, fool! Fool! Where is your learning now? Where, where, where . . ." and he began to cry. "Where is your learning now?" he gasped between sobs.

And then the Bishop knew at last that it was the Lord that he was talking about, and he knew the depth of his terrible blasphemy. The Bishop could not meet those awful eyes again and he stared at the floor until the sobbing subsided.

A long time passed before Jacob had the strength to raise his eyes. Much evil had the Bishop come to know of, for prison is the house of evil, the house of death, and every act of evil tore at his heart like a thorn because he was good, and he was selfless. When he finally did, he was staring directly into the eyes of Kerron who sat watching him with an utter intensity.

"You have committed a great evil," Jacob said at last. "The Lord cannot forgive you for this transgression."

"I went all over the village looking for my little Aalin," said Kerron without acknowledging the words of the Bishop. "To everyone I met I damned the Lord and told them of His weakness. I became His accuser. The people recoiled from my accusations and closed their door to my lamentations. I wandered until I collapsed. The people condemned me. They pointed to me and said: *blasphemer*! They cursed me and chased me away until my hatred for the Lord grew even more."

"Don't you understand?" said Bishop Jacob as if a sudden spark had rekindled his sensibility. "Your sin is unforgivable."

"Unforgivable?" said Kerron from within the darkening shadow. "I'm already in prison. I'm already condemned. Take your precious soul with you and leave me alone."

Bishop Jacob stood up and went to the door. He knocked once very loudly. Then he turned back to Kerron who watched him through the resentment of his own self righteousness. "You need to think about eternity," he said. "Eternity is not about time, Kerron. No, eternity is outside of time, and when time is over and darkness covers the land, eternity remains." Then the door opened and he stepped out into the dimness of the lonely corridor and the door closed behind him.

Before leaving the prison Jacob stopped at the cell of *Issak the Stone*. The Bishop did not know what Issak's crime had been to land him in prison because Issak was as still as a stone and would not talk about his crime. Most prisoners were all too eager to confess to the Bishop their crimes in the hope of eliciting mercy, but not Issak. Verily, Issak was eager to talk, but not about his guilt.

Bishop Jacob stepped into the wretchedness of Issak's cell and was reminded of the terrible incarceration of Paul who spent two years rotting away in a Caesarea prison for casting out a demon before being sent to Rome to be judged by Caesar. His incarceration was cruel and unjust, but even Paul could not save himself and he was beheaded in 68 A.D. How much less of a sinner was Issak? Bishop Jacob took pity on all men.

"Tell me your sin so that I may help you," said Bishop Jacob. "There is no more need of secrecy . . . there is no more reason to hide from the truth, for you have been found guilty."

"I am guilty," answered Issak.

"You are guilty before God," Jacob reiterated.

"Yes, God is my judge," said Issak.

Jacob looked at Issak and was moved to pity by what he saw. No pillar dweller hermit or peregrine saint ever looked so lowly and destitute as Issak looked now. His hair was long and wild. He had not bathed and his skin was thin and crusted with sores. But still there was a look of defiance in his eyes, and that is what disturbed the Bishop most.

"You will never leave this prison if you do not confess and repent," Jacob persisted. "You must accept your guilt."

"It is too horrible for me to contemplate," said Issak with sadness in his voice. "I can never speak of it, for if I were to speak of it . . . it would return to my mind, and that I cannot bear."

Jacob saw a small chance of hope. "It is done," he said. "Whatever you have done can never be undone. If you refuse to acknowledge your sin it does not lessen your sin, and it does not diminish your guilt. But if you declare your sin before God and before the Church, you may be forgiven your sin."

Issak looked into Jacob's eyes and they were sad. "I do not wish to be forgiven," he said. "I wish to suffer."

"But, tell me Issak, how long can you suffer?"

"Until the Lord is satisfied," he replied.

Now Bishop Jacob was angry. "Do you wish to stay here? Do you wish to die here . . . in this prison, alone?"

"All men are alone before God," Issak insisted. "It is not good to hide within the body of Christ, for every man must answer for his own life."

There was nothing Jacob could say to penetrate into the soul of such stubbornness, and he knew it. But he had to try, if only for his own sake.

"Tell me Bishop," said Issak with growing fervor. "Is it true that to God, all sin is equal? This is what I have been taught . . . but if all sin is truly equal to God, and all men are sinners . . . then it is no more sinful to God if one mutilates children than it is to steal a loaf of bread to assuage gnawing hunger. To God all hunger and all need is the same."

"Thoughts like this will not help you," said Jacob.

"But is it true! Is it true?" Issak demanded forcefully.

"All sin separates us from God, that is true," Jacob answered. "The Lord cannot abide sin, for the Lord is sinless. That is why he sacrificed his own flesh and suffered for us."

Issak would not listen to the words of the Bishop and only became more and more despondent.

"But if we love God," he pleaded. "If we truly love God and He lives in our heart . . . then tell me why He would allow Himself to be used for such evil?"

"Do not make the mistake of supposing to use God," Jacob said, still trying to reason with the prisoner's lamentations. "It is God that uses us. No, the plans of the Lord cannot be altered, and what for you is your own free will, is already known to God. This is true."

"That cannot be true!" Issak shouted with rage. "If my will is not my own . . . then, then the terrible things I have done are not my fault, they are the fault of God."

Then Issak was silent and he seemed to be turning a particular thought over in his mind. The Bishop watched him and his heart was moved. Though he looked down on a terrible sinner, the Bishop knew that all men were sinners and the anguish of Issak only made him feel weaker.

"There is a hole in the world," Issak said looking up. "I know where it is because it is right here in my cell. Sometimes I plan to escape. I want to escape that is true. Sometimes I plan to escape . . . but I never do."

"You would do well to alter your plans," said Jacob. "This is where you are and this is where you must be. There are no more plans for you to make, Issak."

Issak smiled. "I know a lot about spiders," he said. "It is true, for I watch them when they come out and I see the things that they do. And I know that the flies come for me because I am unclean . . . Yes, I know that I am unclean and wretched. I cannot bear to smell my own wretchedness . . . But the spiders come to me to get the flies. But, but the spiders do not know that it is I that feeds them, for it is not for them to know. No, the spiders do not know because they hide during the daylight when I am thinking. And I hide during the darkness when the Lord is thinking."

"St. Anthony was often attacked by flies," said Jacob calmly as the words of Issak lulled him into a strange torpor.

"The whole world is like a spider web." Issak continued. "This is what I have discovered. It is true that I am grateful to be here in this prison, for otherwise I never would have known. The web is so thin, so delicate, but we do not see the web, nor do we feel the web as it coils and coils and coils around us. No, no we do not see the web, and even though we are entangled in silk, we never know. This is what I have discovered." Then Issak smiled strangely at the

Bishop. "The spider feels the quivering fly caught in the web, and so the Master must feel our pathetic struggle as we try to tear free, but our struggle only entangles us further as our struggle announces our presence."

"And have you also discovered a way into hell?" asked the Bishop who was growing weary of such speech. "Because if you die here without confessing your sins, then that is where you must go."

"No, I have not thought about that," Issak replied.

"Hell is darker than any darkness that you can ever know."

Issak jerked as a new thought occurred to him. "And you have seen this?" he asked in anticipation.

"No, I have not seen this, Issak. But the Lord has spoken of it, and the saints have been taken there in visions. Eternal darkness, Issak, eternal nothingness, eternal emptiness, an emptiness that is devoid of all thought, all warmth, and all awareness. What would you do? Your cries will never be heard. Think about that, Issak."

"Darkness is not so bad."

"Suffering, Issak! Eternal suffering . . ."

"I am weary, for such talk makes me want to sleep. Would you leave me now?"

Bishop Jacob knew that it was best to leave when a prisoner no longer accepted his presence. Many times he had witnessed as a prisoner would shrink from him until he could not be reached, and had become insensate, but would only stare with blank, vacant watery eyes. The Bishop knew that such was the expression of God's work, and it was best that he not interfere.

Jacob left and rode to Bishopscourt and ate a light meal before retiring to his private garden to meditate. Not overly ornate and symmetrically pleasing like the private garden of King Sigmus, the Bishop's garden offered something different, something quite special: it offered complete solace, and it was during such periods of solace that Jacob came closest to his understanding of the will of the Lord. The calmness brought to his mind by the natural, asymmetric beauty was a form of enchantment.

The private gardens of Bishopscourt were constructed by Bishop Jacob and the many bishops before him that lived and worked from the idyllic location. The Bishop particularly liked a grove of fruit trees that he planted, and he ate from the trees and thought it was good, for beauty without purpose was good, but beauty endowed with a purpose was closer to the divine will of the Lord.

Also of particular interest was the tower, *King Orry's Tower*, as it had come to be known. There are many legends about the tower and its construction, but there are no records and only fragments and old myths and folklore remain. The legend that Bishop Jacob came to love the most went like this:

One day the Great Deceiver decided to pay a visit to the shores of Man. He had heard that a great and honorable King lived there and that his name was King Orry. The Deceiver never tired in his long work of spreading lies and despair and all other forms of mischief, so he was confident that his work should be complete in a day or two.

The Deceiver walked along the quiet lanes and byways and he spoke to the people to know if the rumor be true. The people dutifully admitted that such was the case and that the rumor was true. The Deceiver was not happy, and so he went to the inns and taverns to hear what those people might say. Everyone agreed that King Orry was righteous and that his reign was supreme.

In disguise the Deceiver went to King Orry and offered his fealty for such a righteous and superior king as King Orry. But King Orry responded with consternation, saying that he was dust and that all his works be folly but for the grace of Christ. Now the Great Deceiver reviled that name and so he came to also revile the name of King Orry.

At first the Deceiver haunted the King's dreams, calling forth all manner of lustful and insidious temptations. King Orry however enlisted the power of the Lord and he remained righteous. Next the Deceiver brought forth a legion of dark angels to terrorize the good King Orry. They chased him and drove him across the land all the way to the sea, and that is where King Orry constructed a great stone tower in which to wait out the growing pestilence, for he knew of the Great Deceiver and the evil he could command, but he was not afraid.

The Deceiver brought great serpents and worms, but King Orry brought a great angel with wings. The Deceiver brought forth terrible winds and tempests, but King Orry brought forth a great lion. The Deceiver called up demons and monsters, but King Orry called forth a mighty ox. Next the Deceiver called up a terrible sorceress, but the King called forth an eagle. Now the Deceiver was growing impatient, and that is when he called forth his own very spirit to penetrate into the stone tower.

"Why do you fight against me?" the Deceiver asked King Orry. "Do you not see what a great ally I could be for you?

"You have no right to be here!" King Orry thundered at the wavering apparition. "Leave this place at once!"

"Such a tiny island," the Deceiver remarked thoughtfully. "Imagine . . . how much greater is the entire world. It is within your power should you decide to join forces with me."

"By the power of Christ I command you to go!" the King shouted with such fury that the very walls shook within his rage. Now the captain of the guard, having heard the raging of the King, stormed into the room just as the Deceiver was fading into the black vapor of his presence. And suddenly the Deceiver plunged into the body of the unsuspecting guard, drawing his sword and brandishing it before the King. The two men commenced into a fiery battle, but the King was a much better swordsman and carefully disarmed his loyal captain.

The Deceiver was defeated, but in a last act of desperation the Deceiver jumped out of the open casement window and fell to his death below. King Orry lamented. The power of Christ had saved his people, but the cost had been great. And from that moment forward a formal annual expression of fealty to the power of Christ was taken throughout the realm of King Orry. The tower stands as a powerful symbol of the dominion of the Lord as we should all stand in the righteousness of Christ.

𝕹𝖎𝖌𝖍𝖙 𝖁𝖎𝖌𝖎𝖑𝖘

The darkness of the hopeless passage upward, like a tunnel chiseled into hell, always invoked conflicting thoughts for Jacob, thoughts of thankfulness for the grace he had been given, but also thoughts of utter despair for the many lives that were wasted and lost forever, lives that would end needlessly without hope and without redemption, and ultimately without forgiveness; alas, it was the bitterness in men's hearts that separated them from grace. Bishop Jacob and King Sigmus had been friends for many years, had broken bread together and had shed tears together. The Bishop was there for the King when he lived through his dark nights of the soul, the Bishop knew of the King's faults and the weaknesses, but he also knew that the King was prone to wild flights of fancy and profound insights into the deepest depths of the soul, and for this reason the Bishop rejoiced when the King rejoiced, and lamented when the King lamented.

The day to day operations of the Bishopscourt grounds and structures was done by laypersons and biblical scholars come to Bishopscourt to study. Occasionally the abbot from Rushen Abbey visited and brought along special books to be studied by the Bishop. The main rectory contained many rare and important books. Bishop Jacob spent much of his free time studying the books and the voluminous annotations therein for it was known that the library at Bishopscourt was unique and scholars visited from distant parts, so the guest house was seldom unoccupied.

Dividing his time between Bishopscourt and his beloved Rushen Abbey in Ballasalla, the Bishop tried not to become accustomed to unnecessary luxuries and refinements. The meals at the abbey were rudimentary and without flavor, but they were sufficient and sustaining. He prayed the *hours* when he was at the abbey, and when he was at Bishopscourt he did his best to keep the major *hours* because his heart was tuned to the perfection of such adoration. Seldom did the Bishop eat meat, and though he was no longer bound to the strict rules of the Order of Cistercian monks, he followed the rules of St. Benedict as closely as possible, for in truth, weakening of the body strengthened the spirit.

An iron bell tolled far in the distance. Bishop Jacob was roused gently from his sleep by an acolyte. He liked to keep Matins, for the Lord has given us not only daylight, but also spiritual light of Christ the Savior. He dressed slowly and prepared his mind for the morning worship which would celebrate first light, and so as the sun would always rise on a new day, the light of Christ would be the light of the world.

Later that morning Bishop Jacob rode out to a small hamlet on the edge of his parish in the sheading of Kirk Michael. The villagers were frightened, for it was said that the devil had been sighted. The village priest was then petitioned to come to their aid. The priest, however, sent for the Bishop because he was too frightened to act alone. He waited for Bishop Jacob to arrive, and when he did the priest took his hand eagerly.

"Thank you for coming," he said. "Christ be with you."

"And also with you," Jacob responded.

The priest, whose name was Phillip, was dressed in black cassock and went without a hat. He led Jacob into the rectory where tea was served. Bishop Jacob would have preferred to skip such niceties, but he knew that a visit usually prompted formalities of which he was uncomfortable. The slow moving life on the island left much time for tea and conversation and wild speculation. Jacob was polite and smiled when the priest paused for a moment.

"Tell me," said Jacob, bringing the conversation to the point. "What do you think is troubling the flock?"

Phillip spoke in earnest. "They are terrified of the devil," he said. "At first I was rather dubious of such fears, but the fears only continued to rise up as more and more sightings were reported. In the end, the people came to my door for help . . . that would have been three days past now."

Jacob listened with growing interest. He did not judge the words but only listened carefully. "Tell me Phillip," he said. "What do you believe?"

"The flock knows the smell of a wolf," he said. "I believe that the devil is here. He has often been spotted walking along the road, but he has not come into our midst yet, unless I am mistaken."

"And the people . . . what do they say?"

"The people are afraid to leave their houses, Jacob."

"What does he look like, Phillip? Has anyone seen his face?"

"The people that have seen him will not talk," said Phillip. "Or they cannot talk. In truth, the village is in an uproar and the people are growing suspicious of strangers."

"What will you do?" Jacob asked.

"I sent for you," Phillip responded as if the only thing to be done was now done. "I thought that you would help us."

Jacob thought that Phillip had shown unforgivable weakness, but he did not utter his scornful words. Instead he only asked, "Tell me where I may find this . . . devil, Phillip. I will investigate."

"Take the road to Kirk Michael," Phillip said."You may pass him along the road. I will stay here and pray to the Lord that we not be plagued by pestilence and by demons, for the devil brings pestilence and sows the earth with corpses."

The road to Kirk Michael is no road at all but only a beaten path with a few stones hastily placed like the crumbling ruins of Hadrian's Wall. Few trees and only brush and bracken and wild grass pepper the rocky moorland that follows the western edge of the Irish Sea. Open and desolate, the Bishop liked to come to this part of the island to take in the wildness and beauty, and in truth, such emptiness, such remote sparseness helped him to think.

Up ahead he saw a man standing in the middle of the path. Crows circled above against the leaden sky. The Bishop started to sweat as he increased his gait. The man continued to watch without moving an inch. Jacob looked hard; he squinted to get a clear picture of the man because his image wavered. Above, the crows circled directly over the man. Afraid that the man would disappear altogether, the Bishop walked even faster. The cold air was still, but the man's cloak fluttered as though an unseen tempest surrounded him. Suddenly the Bishop began to run before the apparition should fade, but as the turning whirlwind caught the man and twisted the dust and debris all around him, the man dissolved into the turning vortex. Bishop Jacob rubbed his eyes and tried to fathom what had just happened but his mind would not formulate the words necessary to describe it, for the words in his head were turning even as the whirlwind dissipated. Finally, after a few moments of bewilderment, the Bishop turned around and walked back to the village.

At midnight Jacob was awoken by an acolyte for [4]Vigils of the nocturnal *hours*,

---

[4] *Opus dei*, The Divine Office, has developed through the centuries as a way for the Church to sanctify the work of the Lord in the world in which men live. And so, the hours of the day are divided into canonical *hours* to praise the hours of the day, even as the passion of the

one of three nocturnes of the Night Office. Still shaken by the strange apparition earlier, the Bishop sang the psalms with even greater vibrancy as if the clearness of his voice could bring clearness to his questioning mind.

Later that day the Bishop rode away to talk to the people of his parish where he would determine the level of their fear and decide what to do then. Sitting atop his horse the Bishop looked like a powerful lord. The people respected powerful men and they were in awe of their learning. The soft footfalls of his horse almost put Jacob to sleep and he walked right past a Manxman working in a field that stood and stared as the Bishop rode past. But then suddenly the Bishop pulled back on the reins and looked back at the Manxman who was still scratching his head.

"Good day to you," said the Bishop with a slight inclination of his head.

"Aye," the Manxman responded. "For good or for evil I welcome you, my lord."

"I am Bishop Jacob and I am not your lord. Do you welcome strangers as friends in this village?"

The man looked perplexed by the question, for he was slow to understand. He stared for a moment. "I am a friend of all men," he finally said. "But I am no friend of the Irish . . . or to the devil either," and then he spat.

"Have you seen the devil then?" Jacob asked hastily.

"He wanders to and fro . . . but he never stands still. That is what they say. He is here for a moment and then he is gone . . . and if he should catch your gaze . . ."

"And tell me, my good man, how do you know that this is the devil?"

The man brought his hand to his chin and scratched his face. "One does not easily mistake the devil I think. No, one does not mistake the devil for a potato puller or a caster of nets or a wind worker. The devil is more clever than a Manxman floating above a sea of herring, listening, feeling their slimy slithering ways and casting nets. The devil has no net because the devil is a net. Yes, I hear that the devil is clever."

"You know the devil then?" Jacob asked with excitement. "You have seen him

---

Lord is praised. As such, the Office is performed dutifully by the monks as a sacrifice and to mark the glory of the Lord, for men were commanded to praise the Lord continuously.

before?"

"Don't know nothing," the man replied nervously. "Don't want to know nothing. Aint seen the devil and I aint seen the Lord. If you see the Lord . . . tell him to come here 'cause we need him."

The Story of Barabbas

"There is evil abound that cannot abide the image of man," Sigmus said. "The image of man was cast in the image of the Lord, and that is why our very presence evokes the greatest indignation from fallen angels and wicked men."

"Yes, that is true," Bishop Jacob answered. "But it is equally true that the image of the Lord has been put into the heart of all men, and but for the separation caused by eternal sin should abide forever."

"Yes Jacob, that is likewise true. And it may be true that the thorns that have pierced the heart of men are more painful to the Lord than the thorns that were thrust upon His own head."

Jacob rode along the well-trodden road back to the abbey feeling miserable. He was troubled by his visit to the prison. As the sky darkened, his thoughts began to darken. His visits to the prison often left him feeling troubled, but his present apprehension was brought about by a completely different manifestation of grief. Many of the prisoners he had visited over the years had committed heinous acts of murder and brutality, but after spending time in the prison they would begin to accept their guilt. The hardness of the prison often softened the hardest heart. These men, even though they be ostracized from their fellow men, had hope of redemption and of finally reaching the blessed gates of heaven. These men often became quiet and sullen and thoughtful in the face of such severe isolation, for as water eats through rock, bitter isolation eats through the hardest shell of a man; all men live in shells and in the end, all these shells are cracked open. Men such as these often turned to God when they had no one else to turn to. He knew that Kerron had turned from God when he needed Him most, and he feared that when his shell was cracked open there would be nothing left inside.

Along the western edge of the cloister, closest to the watchtower, Bishop Jacob kept a small cell within the community of lay brothers who were not themselves entitled to individual cells. His cell was small, devoid of useless amenities, and meagerly furnished with a few sticks of furniture and a comfortable chair from which to study the large folios and transcripts privately in the afternoon sunlight. The Bishop was entitled to much better quarters, but the Cistercians are known for such simplicity, and he adamantly refused and would not further elaborate on the matter. Yes, the Bishop was a man of simple means and his humility was known across the island.

When Jacob entered his cell after vespers where he would wait for night prayer, he sat down at the window and closed his eyes for a moment. He was fatigued and said a silent prayer asking for strength. In truth, the sin of Kerron bound him and he could not let it go. Jacob knew that while all men sin, not all me suffer their sins to be forgiven; he had seen it before and it was always troublesome for him, for evil is the man who is fortified by his own sin.

Early the next day, Bishop Jacob rode out to speak with Sigmus. The King was seated at a small desk tucked into an alcove window where he liked to sit in the mornings reading, in the bright sunlight. When Jacob entered, the King stood up and took his hand warmly. Then he led him into another room and offered him to be seated. Tea was served and the King ate hungrily the sweet confections, but the Bishop refused and took only a single cup of tea.

"Good morning Jacob," he said. "What brings you here today?"

"I have recently been to the prison," he answered. "There I spoke with *Kerron the Blasphemer* . . ."

The Bishop stopped and looked into the eyes of his friend, trying to gauge their empathy. King Sigmus was empathetic, of that the Bishop knew without doubt and the King's pale blue watery eyes betrayed his sometimes feeble attempts to disguise them with harshness. For a few moments only the sound of the King's breathing and the soft chirping of a tiny wren perched on an overhanging bough outside the open window could be heard. The King looked up and waited for the Bishop to continue.

"I was very moved by his story," Jacob continued.

"As was I," Sigmus agreed calmly.

"So you remember him?" Jacob said with cautious surprise, as if he were reticent to mention it at all.

The King focused his gaze on his friend. "I do not forget those whom I condemn."

"His punishment from God will be severe, Sigmus. Must his punishment on Earth also be severe?"

The King pursed his lips as if trying to hold back a thought that was trying to come out. He said only, "After all these years, do you still question my judgment?"

Jacob blushed slightly. "No, I do not question your judgment, Sigmus. But I thought that perhaps you had forgotten him."

"Is the sin of blasphemy of no concern of yours then?" Sigmus said.

"All sin is my concern," Jacob answered with confidence. "No man is without sin . . . that is true."

"All men, Jacob?" Sigmus asked with purpose.

"We are born into sin, Sigmus. You know this to be true."

The King sighed impatiently. "And there is forgiveness of sin . . ."

"Yes, there is forgiveness," Jacob answered decisively without waiting for the King to finish speaking.

"Not for blasphemy!" the King shouted with such vigor that the Bishop jumped in his seat.

Startled by the unexpected intensity of the King, and trying to bring the conversation to more agreeable topics, Jacob said, "How is Iona, Sigmus? Is she still with you?"

Sigmus, however, mistook the intention of his friend's expression and answered curtly, "So now we are talking about my sins, Jacob?"

"I have been praying for his soul," the Bishop said, bringing the conversation back to the reason for his visit. "I cannot believe that he can be condemned for eternity."

The King thought a moment before saying, "And his story . . . he told it to you?"

"Yes," Jacob answered readily. Then he proceeded to relate to the King what he had been told. When he was finished speaking he waited to hear what the King would say.

Sigmus shook his head doubtfully. "There is more," he said, "much more. I am afraid that the blasphemer did not finish the story, Jacob. It should serve you well that you should go to him and ask him to finish the story. Perhaps you will understand my actions more thoroughly when you have heard the tale of the blasphemer."

"I will do that," answered Jacob. "But tell me, Sigmus. The prisoner at the top in the tower . . . what has he done?"

"Why do you ask?" Sigmus answered uneasily as if annoyed at the question and wishing the Bishop would desist from further questioning.

"I would like to speak with him, Sigmus. I was told, however, that it was forbidden by you."

"I will not allow it," Sigmus said perfunctorily. Then he softened a bit because of his fondness for the Bishop. "My respect for you is great my friend, but I will not allow it."

"Can you at least tell me why?" Jacob said respectfully but with purpose. He had never known Sigmus to be hard and overbearing, so he was slightly perplexed by his demeanor.

"It is my desire that this man may never again see the light of day."

Bishop Jacob was pained by the words of his friend. "All men deserve a second chance," he said with conviction.

"Spoken like a true man of God. Do not try to persuade me, Jacob. You and I are friends. I owe you much. In truth, it was you that helped bring me back to life, but I cannot allow you to see this man."

"Will you tell me what his crime was, Sigmus? Can you at least tell me why he has been incarcerated in such a horrible and woeful place?"

"It is not for what he has done," the King said unexpectedly. "It is for what he may do."

"But surely he has done something!" Jacob cried with passion. "Sigmus, surely you did not condemn him without reason."

Finally the King relented and told Jacob the truth. "Do you believe in sorcery?" he began.

"The bible speaks of sorcerers and witches. Are you telling me that you have a sorcerer locked away in prison?"

"I would have him killed," Sigmus said gravely, "but for what he may do then. He shall remain locked away until his bones dissolve in the salty air, for that is the only way to be rid of him."

Jacob sat in silence and contemplated the words of the King. He dare not ask the King for more. Instead, he only lifted the cup to his lips and drank the remaining tepid tea. The King watched his friend and was moved by his selfless compassion. For several minutes both men sat in silence, waiting for the other to speak. Finally, after the atmosphere was becoming oppressive, Jacob spoke, for a new thought had entered his mind.

"If he is a sorcerer, then tell me why he has not escaped from his cell. Would he not have escaped by now, Sigmus?"

"Do you doubt my words again, Jacob?"

"You have said that he is a sorcerer and that is good enough for me. But tell me, Sigmus . . . have you proof of such an assertion? Would not a sorcerer, a true sorcerer, have escaped by now? I have heard tales of sudden transmogrifications."

Finally the King yielded. His expression changed and by degrees he became more thoughtful and even more dour and more serious. He wiped his mouth. Then he dropped his napkin on the plate and leaned back in his chair.

"Alright," he said to Jacob, "Since you persist with such passion I will tell you why Barabbas was condemned." Then the King told his story:

"There was a time when Barabbas was a good man, and never would he have committed an evil act. In the south, on a cliff overlooking the sea, he lived with his loyal wife and their small boy Eliakim, which means *whom God will raise up*.

"Barabbas earned his living from the wool he gathered from sheep and from what he was able to salvage from the sea. Yes, his income was modest, but his soul was also modest because his thought was for his family and that there would always be enough food.

"One day a small sheep wandered too close to the precipice. Barabbas saw the sheep but he knew that he could not reach it in time. His young son, however, was tending the sheep and ran to save it. He went too close to the edge sadly and plummeted over the edge and was killed. Barabbas saw what was happening, but he could not reach his boy in time to save him. In vengeance Barabbas took the sheep which had survived and hurtled it into the abyss, into the surging sea to be smashed upon the rocks.

"But that was not the end of his woe. Overcome with grief, the poor man's wife Lael, which means *belonging to God*, took her own life soon after. Now Barabbas was utterly alone. He looked to God for comfort but became more and more despondent, for God was either not listening, or He was not speaking . . .

The Bishop raised an eyebrow, but said nothing. His heart was moved and he waited for an end to the story though he was not hopeful.

"Barabbas prayed day and night. He prayed continuously, for his heart was broken, but still God would not speak to him. Next, Barabbas decided to fast so that he could prove his love for the Lord . . . but the Lord did not speak to him.

"One day, early in the morning when a fine mist rose up from the sea, Barabbas decided to cast his own body into the abyss so great was his own grief. Then, walking amongst his blessed sheep, he moved closer and closer to the edge and to his doom. The urge to end his life was so powerful and it pushed him even closer to the abyss and to the end of his pain. He said no prayer that morning. Instead, he only moved closer to the edge as he closed his eyes . . .

'And that is when the Lord finally spoke to him?' Bishop Jacob interrupted eagerly.

"He jumped," Sigmus answered dolefully.

Bishop Jacob opened his mouth to speak but said nothing for he was surprised. This was completely unexpected.

"Barabbas was saved that day, Jacob. But not by the Lord . . . that day he was saved by the devil."

Bishop Jacob nearly jumped out of his chair. "Surely this cannot be true!" he cried. He could not believe what he was hearing, and he spoke as much to confirm his own faith than to question the word of the King. "The Lord would never allow such a thing to happen, dear Sigmus. Pray tell me, who told you this story?"

"Barabbas told me this story," Sigmus said with conviction, "just before I locked the door and left him to rot."

"I still do not understand," Jacob said. "Surely you have not locked him away in prison because you believe he was saved by the devil. The people believe many things that are far stranger than this, but you do not lock them away. Tell me Sigmus, what is the reason?"

"Trust me when I tell you that Barabbas is a dangerous man, Jacob. If he were to escape, the terror and destruction that he could wield are too terrible to imagine."

Bishop Jacob shifted uncomfortably in his chair. "He is just a man, Sigmus."

"He is now fortified with the power and the cunning of the devil. The devil has called, and Barabbas has answered. Yes, Jacob, the man locked behind that prison door is no longer Barabbas, for Barabbas has died . . . and has now been reborn in the image of the devil."

Bishop Jacob gasped.

"The devil is clever Jacob. The devil deals in souls . . . as does the Lord. With great satisfaction it must have been to have the soul of Barabbas fall literally into his hands."

"You know this to be true, Sigmus?"

The King continued to speak and did not hear the protestations of his friend. "There were rumors about this man, Barabbas. I heard many stories brought to me by frightened Manxmen and local deemsters. The stories were too difficult for me to believe, and that is what attracted my attention. The people were truly frightened. That is when I decided to pay a visit to this unfortunate man, Barabbas:"

On a very cold morning just after the [5]Feast of Purification, I rode south to the village of Cregneash, home to the great four horned Loagtan sheep, just south of Port Erin, to see Barabbas. I was aware of his terrible loss and I wanted to console him if I could. Though I knew that his tragedy had happened before midsummer's eve, I also knew that time was irrelevant when the time of grief was nigh and I knew that grief was the mother to self destruction.

A light snow had fallen during the night and a thin crust covered the hard ground.

---

[5] Feast of Purification: Candlemas Day, The Church tried to transfer festivities from the 1st to the 2nd to eliminate the memory of Brigid. Hence many customs are the same on the two days.

The air was thick and my horse snorted clouds of steam as we picked our way up the steep slope to the cliff where the stone cottage of Barabbas was perched up against the cold sea. White smoke curled from his fireplace and I could smell the rich resin of burning wood.

He came out of his cottage to meet me even before I had dismounted. Tall, gaunt, he was completely dressed in black, the color of mourning and grief. On his fingers I could see tiny flickers of light as it reflected the sunlight and sent slivers flying. He smiled and I assumed that he must have known who I was. Holding out his hand he said:

"Welcome. My name is Barabbas. Tell me what business you have with me and what is your name."

"I am King Sigmus," I said. "My business is with a man named Barabbas. If you are Barabbas, then my business is with you."

He stopped smiling the moment I told him my name, and it is true that he did not expect me. His black eyes narrowed as he watched me and tried to guess my mission.

"I have heard the story of your recent tragedy Barabbas, and I want to tell you how sad I was to hear it. I would like to help you if you are in need of help."

To my surprise, he smiled again as if he were amused by my offer of help. I was slightly repulsed by his smile for it was the smile of one with something to hide, the smile of one with a secret, the slightly curled lip of a jeweler, but I said nothing.

"Yes, it is a pity that I could not save her," he said curtly.

"And your boy . . . ?"

He looked down. "I have warned him often about the dangerous cliff."

"You have lost much," I said to him, trying to fathom his extraordinary detachment from so recent a tragedy. His demeanor was philosophical when I expected to find a broken man suffering from an emotional upheaval.

"What is lost is in the past," he said flatly. "What is in the past is over, and to live in the past is to die. I do not wish to die."

"Is there anything I can do for you?" I asked, even as my compassion was turning to antipathy.

He looked at me with surprise and for several moments appeared about to speak. Finally he said.

"I have no more desire to tend sheep for I loathe them now. The sight of them sickens me. Will you take them?"

"I will give you a fair price."

Distracted, he looked up. His eyes were glassy and cold as the eyes of a crow. "For what?" he answered.

A week later I came back to see him again. It was my intention to make him an offer for his sheep. He looked at me strangely.

"I no longer have them," he said.

"What happened to them?" I asked with surprise.

"They are gone," he said without explanation.

I could feel that he was waiting for me to leave and that I had interrupted him. Again, he was wearing the same black clothes. I looked into his eyes; they were vacant and seemed to look right through me without seeing, or as if he were seeing something that existed beyond me. The pause was becoming awkward. Finally I asked him.

"I hope that you received a fair price for them."

Annoyed by my persistence he answered, "That does not concern me. My work is all that concerns me now."

By way of apology I said, "Our work brings us closer to God."

He smiled uncontrollably and his smile brought me to sudden anger. "Do you find that to be amusing?" I asked tersely.

"But for the Lord, we would not have to work at all . . . but work we must."

"But for the Lord," I shot back at him uncomfortably, "we would fall prey to the devil and all his demons."

"Perhaps," he said cryptically, "Perhaps not."

Later that day after the sun had gone down I returned to the cottage of Barabbas. It was dark but for the glow of a light shining weakly through his window. As a king, I knew that it was my right to be there, but still I felt awkward and ashamed as if I was doing something shameful. In truth, his behavior had so distressed me that I had to find out his secret, for I was convinced that he hid an awful secret.

Leaving my horse tied to a tree away from sight, I carefully and stealthily approached his cottage, a thing easily done for I was a hunter of no small ability. Dressed in black, I wanted to be inconspicuous, for I had no desire to be discovered lurking around in the darkness of a man so recently crushed by tragedy; kings were supposed to have a retinue of minions for doing such things.

Peering through his window, I was aghast by what I saw happening inside only a few feet away. In the center of the room there stood Barabbas, dressed in black as before. He was standing in the center of a large circle traced on the floor with chalk, and surrounded with lit candles placed along the circumference of the circle at the intersections, reminding me of a compass rose. I was familiar with the Hermetic circle and the circle of Solomon, but this circle was different, more sinister looking. The circle was divided into divisions of six, and then further subdivided into areas of twelve, connected with lines that rendered the circle into geometric form. Along the circumference and connecting the cardinal points were symbols that looked runic or Egyptian in origin, but I was unfamiliar and only saw them for a moment so I did not have time to decipher the esoteric meaning.

Barabbas held a book from which he was reading. He spoke with careful attention and his mouth formed the words slowly, but I could not hear the words, or my ears would not comprehend the arcane speech. From what secret magic he called I could not guess, but I knew that he was invoking something old, something dangerous and evil, and that such evil had existed during the times of Enoch even before God destroyed the Earth with torrential rain to wash away sinners and begin anew. And now the room began to darken as a thick layer of mist swept across the floor. Suddenly the opaque mass lifted, obscuring the body of Barabbas. Round and round the thickening mass rotated around the body of Barabbas, touching him, guiding him, immersing him in the torrent of evil until he was disappeared.

I ran around to the front of the cottage and, with a tremendous kick, broke the door in. The mass was still rotating as if held to the spot by powerful sorcery. The pungent smell of fire filled the air. Now my ears could feel the force and the pain mounted. Then, without thinking clearly, I jumped into the turning miasma . . . and then I too was gone.

Darkness closed in all around me, enveloping me in a warm, tight cocoon. I could feel pressure, the presence of an amorphous, wraithlike substance that prickled my skin. And I could feel the presence of something else . . . emptiness and prevailing loneliness that only became more acute the longer I stood there. Then I moved and discovered that I was no longer in the cottage of Barabbas, but that by some stupefying magic I had been transported to another place. After a few paces I stopped as the horror washed over me like a wave of doom. I could not move. Terror froze me to the spot. What place was this? Now the sweet scent in my nostrils had become rank and I knew that I had come to a very bad place.

The darkness was so complete that I no longer experienced my own existence but through my mind. Turning completely around I looked for any sign of light, but the darkness was absolute. I turned and turned until I lost my balance and fell to the floor. Cold to the touch, it seemed to be made of solid rock. I tried to stand up and fell down again for my balance had no orientation, nothing with which to stabilize my intellect.

Now my head was reeling, because with nothing to hold on to, nothing to anchor me, I was floating away into a void. I jumped to my feet: "Where are you?" I shouted.

The sound of my voice was very thin, being absorbed into the nothingness like forgotten memories or an echo into an endless well. Instinctively my hand went for the silver pommel of my sword and the solidity gave me comfort and cleared my mind. I knew that Barabbas was here and that he had followed the devil into this hellish domain, but now I too was trapped.

I searched the pockets of my waistcoat and my fingers came around the stem of my pipe. Drawing the pipe from my coat I searched for a match, and striking it across my thumbnail a tiny spark, which coming out of such total darkness seemed like an explosion, lit up the darkness around me. Holding the match across the bowl of my pipe, the flame intensified and I could see further into the murky darkness. All around me was a cavernous, mountainous landscape of barren isolation, and I thought that even the moon could not be more barren or more lonely if ever I were to go there. Of course this was Hell or some hellish separation, I knew this for where else could I possibly be? Barabbas had followed the devil, and I had followed Barabbas . . . into Hell.

Alone, sent into perdition like the fallen angels, I felt pity for the lonely souls cast away, devoured by the darkness, banished and forced to live apart from God. Yes, I could literally feel the pain of loneliness as a palpable, visceral gnawing in my very substance. But as of yet, I had no experience of or awareness of those for whom I felt such pity, for I felt only dull, vague pain and not the sharpness that could bring me back into the world of matter. So I smoked my pipe and I started walking.

Soon I began to sense that the path was leading downward, for I was walking through a narrow passageway that was beaten down by the soft tread of many feet and not unlike a road. The sound of my own footfalls was muffled, but I knew that the surface was solid and unchangeable and not part of nature. I also became aware of a faint light coming from below and that I could see partially through the shadows which were now made even darker and more ominous by the light.

A long time I walked until I became distracted by a mournful sound . . . it was the sound of weeping. Then I saw a man dressed in a long, unclean, woolen robe, leaning against a rock, covering his face with his hands, and I could hear his terrible weeping and his body trembled weakly. I walked right up to him, but through his terrible lamentations he could not hear me. Reaching out I touched his arm. The weeping stopped long enough for him to look up, but then he continued weeping despite my presence.

"Why are you weeping?" I asked softly but boldly. "My name is King Sigmus. What place is this?"

He looked at me and his eyes were wet with tears, frozen tears that would never thaw. His face was pale and lifeless, drained of all substance by years of bitter weeping.

"Why do you not weep?" he cried between sobs. "Can you not feel it? Are you so devoid of pity that you can endure such anguish unmoved?"

"What are you talking about?" I asked.

"Such utter loneliness, endless, continuous, never ending, never abating until the end of time. Years are like moments and moments are endless successions of remorse . . . how can you bear it?"

"Are you dead?" I finally asked.

"There is no death," he cried. "There is only life, and the hope of death."

"Tell me, did you see another man such as myself? He was dressed in black."

He raised his head wearily. "You are the first man I have seen since my time here began . . . one long night it has been."

Then he resumed his terrible weeping and I had to leave him to his own misery and his wailing faded away in the distance. I walked for a long time and the way was always downward. Cavernous and gloomy, a faint red glow permeated the suffocating darkness. Every step took me further away from where I began, but curiosity drove me onward.

I finally found him hiding in a forest. Unlike any forest I had ever seen, this was a forest of dead, petrified and lifeless trees. A strange fruit hung off of some of the denser boughs, resembling twisted limbs and torsos more than the fruit of a fig or other eatable food. The trees were close together like rotting corpses in a common grave, and with an unsettling feeling I entered. Revulsion rose up within me and I felt anger along with deep, mournful pity. I also felt shame, but it was not for something that I had done but instead, shame for something that could not be undone. The trees wriggled and writhed as I passed them and I had the impression that they recoiled from me as if the shame belonged to them. I could not understand this eerie feeling and I wanted only to be gone from this forest of despair. And then I saw him. He was sitting beneath one of the trees, and he was weeping. This discovery startled me and I was unprepared for *what I would do next.*

I drew my sword and charged him as if to cut him down. The strong reaction to his presence surprised me. He suddenly looked up at me just as I was about to plunge the sword into his heart. He was still weeping and he did nothing to thwart my attack and prevent his own imminent death. I stopped myself in horror.

"Stand up!" I shouted, for I had no intention of murdering a helpless man. Even less did I want to see him go to his death like one of his sheep.

He stood up as ordered, but then he suddenly turned his back on me and faced the tree again fearlessly. I threw down my sword and grabbed him from behind. Then I pummeled him with my fists until he was knocked senseless. Finally, I picked him up and hoisted him up onto my shoulders, turned, and then walked back the way I had come.

Finally, I remember waking up inside of his cottage. I was still inside of the circle and Barabbas was laying face down next to me. My anger had not subsided. I carried him out to my horse and threw him over the saddle. Then I rode swiftly to the Bishop's Prison and locked him inside. As a King, I answer to no man, and I make no excuses for my severe punishment.

Long after Bishop Jacob was gone the King sat alone in quiet contemplation. The King hated sorcery in all its forms, that is true, but the world was saturated in sorcery and even his tiny island was filled with such evil. The Lord alone claimed the right to such magic and the Lord had forbidden the use of such practices, for the Bible was filled with warnings and admonitions against its use. But King Sigmus was troubled . . . the saints had routinely wielded such power in service to the Lord, that is also true. It was given to the saints to perform every miracle the Lord had also performed, and some of the miracles even exceeded those performed by the Lord: It was given to the saints to call the dead back from the grave; the Dominican priest, Saint Vincent, had even resurrected a dead man to testify to the innocence of another man condemned to die and had offered him the gift of life once more; St. Ambrose levitated while he preached so great was his spirit; the saints had stilled storms, called the wind, multiplied food, walked through solid doors, traveled great distances through the air, and many other miracles. Sigmus worried that for men to perform such miracles, even in service to the Lord, was to usurp the power of the Lord and that even the most devout of men were capable of sin, and that is why sorcery should never be used.

Iona, the King's personal servant, stepped into the grotto with a tray carrying wine and goat's milk cheese. No longer young, she was still beautiful and the lines on her face were etched from the shared grief she felt for the King and for the Lady Kathryn whom she also loved. And now her devotion to the King was complete and her love for him made stronger because of his goodness. Iona was much more to King Sigmus, however, than just a servant and in truth her service was closer to the devotion of a partner. And it is also true that the King reciprocated this devotion. Since the death of Queen Kathryn, Sigmus looked to his devoted servant for comfort and understanding. In return, the King gave her his affection, his love, and his attention. Let no one ever dare accuse the King of impropriety . . . and no one did.

"I've brought you some wine," she said with a smile. "I thought you were relaxing, so I decided to surprise you."

"Thank you, Iona," said King Sigmus. "You are too kind to me."

Iona smiled again. "It was good to see Bishop Jacob," she said. "Were the two of you discussing important matters, or was he just here on a visit?"

"To Jacob, all matters are important," Sigmus answered. Then he said, "I am not in the mood for wine just now, Iona. Why don't you sit down and take a glass for yourself and I will tell you a story."

Iona was only too happy to comply, for it had been a long time since last Sigmus had told her a story. Sigmus was a storyteller that is true, and she loved them all. So she took a glass of wine and sat down on the bench next to Sigmus. Then she smiled and kissed him on the cheek.

"I'm ready now," she announced. "Are you going to scare me again, my love?"

King Sigmus took her small hand and kissed it lightly. The years of work had not destroyed her beautiful hands and he loved to feel them against his face. Then he began.

"Once there was an angel in heaven, a very special angel. This angel was the most beautiful of all the angels, perfect in every way, and the angel served the Lord with great pride and with great joy. All the other angels looked up to this angel because it was favored by the Lord. But this angel was ashamed by the pride that it felt to be so loved by the other angels and by the Lord, and the angel tried to remain humble and servile for it was a mighty angel indeed, it was an archangel.

"The Lord, however, is all powerful and all knowledgeable and the Lord can love many creatures and many things together and at the same time. And even though this angel was special to the Lord because it was more beautiful and more wise and more intelligent than all the other messengers, it was able to love only the Lord. The pride it was to be so favored only increased, for to be in the presence of the Lord was divine.

"One day the Lord sent His angels down to Earth to serve His needs and to admire His new creature — *man*. Made in His own image, the Lord looked upon man and it was good. So the Lord sent His messenger angels to serve the needs of man as if they were the needs of the Lord. And so the Lord's favorite angel was also sent to Earth, but this angel refused to serve the needs of man. Indeed, this mighty angel would only serve the needs of the Lord, for men were inferior and men were beneath the praise of an angel so beautiful and so favored by the Lord."

Sigmus looked up unexpectedly. Then he looked into the eyes of Iona and asked.

"Do you know the name of this angel, Iona?"

Iona smiled. She blushed, for her love for Sigmus was complete. Then she shook her head.

"How could I ever know such a thing?"

"The angel's name is Lucifer," Sigmus said gravely.

"No, no," Iona replied. "Lucifer is the devil."

"Yes Iona, Lucifer is the devil. Lucifer is the angel that was cast out of heaven and thrown down into the abyss. Lucifer and a third of all the angels were fallen, thrown down into the pit. And do you know what Lucifer's great sin was, Iona?"

"He disobeyed the Lord," Iona answered.

"Lucifer's great sin was pride, Iona. Yes indeed, Lucifer however was not proud of his own beauty though he was beautiful beyond the beauty of all the other angels. Lucifer was not proud of his own wisdom even though one third of all the messenger angels followed him into the pit."

"Then what?" Iona asked softly.

"Lucifer was proud of his great love for the Lord, and in his singular, great love, he refused to humble himself before man and before the Lord, for so great was his love that it shone within him like light, like pure radiance, illuminating his great love. We are not to fall in love with our own righteousness, Iona, for all righteousness belongs to the Lord. Lucifer loved his own love more than the Lord, and so he came to love only himself."

"Oh, tell me what to think," Iona said with humility, for she felt great remorse though she could not say why. "Oh, Sigmus, tell me what to believe and I will believe it, because I believe in you."

Days passed normally and the King resumed his business: meeting with Deemsters, drawing up new laws, collecting taxes, and riding throughout his great land speaking to the good people of Man. The King trained with his falcons and hunted quail and spent much time sitting in his garden contemplating the words of other men's words and his own words. He visited with local fishermen in Castletown, he rode into the hills to meet with hermits, he spoke with stonemasons and priests, horsemen, ploughmen, butchers and thieves, for the duties of a King were numerous and broad.

The Devil's Harvest

The first door they passed was reserved for prisoners that were sick unto death and not expected to last long in the brutal conditions. Jacob passed this door and silently said a prayer for the man languishing on the other side of it, for he had met this man and he knew this man, and though he could not save him, he still prayed that his passage into hell would be swift and painless.

Visions of angels were reported across the parish. Many Manxmen, young and old, had reported seeing beautiful creatures bathed in light, descending to Earth. The angels spoke with people and then would just as quickly ascend back into the heavens; later the startled Manxmen would not remember the words of the angel and it would take the use of strong drink to get anything out of them at all.

Jacob visited the people of his parish faithfully and listened to their tales. He asked many questions, but mostly his questions were too difficult for the good Manxmen to answer, for the mind of the Bishop was clear and the mind of the Bishop penetrated into regions of the mind not often contemplated by the good people of his parish.

One day Bishop Jacob was sent for by envoys of the King. He was brought to a small cottage north of Peel where a strange incident had occurred during the previous day. Murder was not unheard of on the isle, but when it happened it was much talked about and it was much thought about. The men would discuss it in the taverns and the women would discuss it in the fields and across clotheslines and in the smelly fish markets. Mostly the good people of Man had no reason for committing murder, and that is why it rarely happened. Ask a Manxman for his shirt and he would give you his trousers, and that is the way it was. Prosperity was shared and grief was also shared, and it was a bitter Manxman that would refuse to help when help was called for.

Bishop Jacob stepped out of the cart in which he was riding and stood in front of the cottage. It was a modest, whitewashed cottage with four windows, a thatched roof, and a flowerbox out of which dying and wilted buttercups grew. The shutters were thrown open and the cream colored curtains fluttered in the breeze. Several men were standing around talking; some of the men were whispering. Jacob recognized with surprise the magnificent steed of the King, and he wondered what could have prompted such a visit.

In a moment King Sigmus emerged from within along with a local deemster named Michelson who had personally informed the King earlier that morning. The King's face showed concern and it is true that he was fairly shaken by what he had just seen. He was looking down. Michelson was holding his arm slightly and speaking carefully into his ear. When he saw the Bishop he stopped speaking. The King looked up.

"Ah, Jacob . . . I thank you for coming so quickly," he said without emotion.

Jacob nodded slightly. "I came as soon as word reached me. Tell me Sigmus, what has happened?"

Michelson started to speak but the King raised his hand and silenced him with a look. "There has been a murder," he said. "This is no ordinary murder however, Jacob. I sent for you so that you should see what has happened, but I warn you . . ."

"Yes, I was told that there was a death," Jacob replied. "I was not told anything else about it though."

"That was my fault," said Michelson. "I told them to ask you to come, but I also told them not to reveal the reason. That was to spare you from filling your mind with terrible thoughts uselessly until you should see for yourself. I hope that you are not too upset."

"You did as I would have done," Jacob replied. "It does no good to dwell on such dark matters of the soul."

King Sigmus spoke up. "Listen Jacob," he said as he placed his hand on the Bishop's shoulder in a comforting way. "This will be difficult for you to see, but it was my wish that you should see for yourself. Later, after you have seen, I will tell you why I sent for you." Then the King turned and escorted Jacob into the cottage.

When the Bishop entered the cottage he understood why the shutters had been thrown open. The stench of death was in the air and his hand instinctively covered his mouth. A few quick steps brought him to the entrance of the sleeping chamber. Sigmus looked back briefly before entering. Jacob followed closely.

His eyes were drawn to the center of the room where a corpse lay atop a small bed like a tableau in death. The blankets were pulled up to the neck like one that was sleeping. Bishop Jacob's eyes went directly to the head and the shock made him wince. The man's face had been burned off and the skin was melted away and curled as it had dissolved. The eyes had been burned out and only two dark, liquid holes remained where they had once been. Fragments of flesh hung from patches of white bone and red, sinewy, burned muscles. All the matter that had once been a face was against the bed sheets where it had collected into a mass of gore. Bishop Jacob looked at the scene and the horror rose within him like a fever.

"What has happened here?" he asked, and his voice trembled slightly.

King Sigmus took hold of Jacob's arm gently and pushed him back a step. Then he took hold of his other arm and turned him away from the death scene. The King was a compassionate man, but he was also a wise man, and he never did anything without a reason, however obscure that reason may be.

"He was killed by his wife," the King said. "He was scalded to death with boiling pitch as he slept. I believe that it was a quick death, Jacob."

"How do you know this?" Jacob asked. "Have you spoken with the woman?"

"She is dead also," the King responded. "She took her own life, Jacob."

The Bishop pursed his lips and contemplated before speaking, for he was badly shaken and did not want to reveal the degree of his shock, for in truth he was horrified. "I will pray for her," Jacob responded the only way he knew how.

Then Sigmus led Jacob to a small room in the farthest corner of the cottage. "You must look at this," he said softly.

There on the floor, with her back leaning against the wall, were the crumpled remains of the woman. A long knife protruded from her chest where it had been plunged in with a strong hand. A small pool of blood formed around her corpse.

"Look at her hands," Sigmus said firmly.

They were burned black. The hands were so severely burned that the flesh was completely burned away in spots. A rank smell of burned flesh wafted from her body.

"She carried the burning pitch with her own hands," Sigmus said with disbelief. "Does that sound like the act of a rational woman, Jacob? Does that sound like the act of one who seeks only to murder? Consider what you see here Jacob and tell me what this means."

Jacob stared at the dead woman and his eyes focused upon her eyes which were still open. A tear started to form in his own eye.

"This makes no sense to me, Sigmus. This is an act of utter despair. I do not understand."

"Let us leave this place," Sigmus said as he led the Bishop away.

They walked out of the cottage together and out of hearing range of the men who still waited for instructions from the King. On a small outcrop of rock they faced the sea and the breeze cooled their faces. For a moment neither man spoke. With a heavy heart Sigmus broke the silence.

"I want you to visit Barabbas," he said finally. "I want you to go to the prison and speak with him. You have my permission."

The First Visit

The King carried a whale-oil lamp and pushed the shadows forward inside a tiny wake of yellow light as they walked. With each step the sound of each footfall on the dirty stone made an ominous, scrapping sound and to the Bishop, the sound was the sound of a doom which was terrible and unstoppable and inexorable, and he was reminded of his first visit to Barabbas.

For several days Bishop Jacob prayed, for his heart was heavy with trepidation. Much time he spent at the abbey, deep in meditation, for the discipline of the *hours* helped prepare his mind. He prayed fervently, and his prayer brought him solace, but he did not yet visit the prison. The death that he had seen left him badly shaken by the sheer savagery involved; the useless taking of life always made him sad. Death prevented repentance, for sin that had not been atoned for in life could never be forgiven, and to die in sin was to forever be separated from God. Many people it is true have died unexpectedly and prematurely, but there was something very different about this one, and in truth it began to haunt his dreams at night . . . and he began to remember his early days as a wandering peregrine and how he was driven from the world of men across the sea into the arms of the Church.

On the fifth day he went to visit Barabbas. Jacob needed no special communication from the King, no signed and sealed document to convince Stephan to allow him access to the prisoner; if Bishop Jacob said it was so, then it was so. Stephan the Keeper did not even see cause to go to the cell with the Bishop to open it, for he wanted little to do with the man behind those doors; he merely gave Jacob the key and warned him to stay back from the second door to avoid possible danger, for there were two doors that guarded Barabbas. With two iron doors to penetrate, the possibility of escape was nil. In truth, the only escape any prisoner ever made was through an iron trapdoor that opened on the floor of the lower, darker region of the tower; the body would be carried out to sea with the tide, and the fishes and other lurking creatures of the sea would complete the job of utterly eliminating any trace of the former prisoner.

Carrying a small lamp to light his way through the darkness, Bishop Jacob began his slow ascent of the tower. Thin key-lights let in some light from outside, but the circular stairwell was mostly dark, mostly cast in shadow, and the small lamp only pushed back the darkness like a small wake through the underworld. Around the inside of the tower the stairwell spiraled up, higher and higher to the top, and along the way iron doors defined each level of the prison behind which an unfortunate soul slowly perished. Jacob went past all these doors, doors behind which men slowly disintegrated in the darkness, for the way was a trail of loneliness. Past these doors he went and he tried to focus his attention on the subject of his current visit. The passage was very narrow and very steep and it was important that one guide their steps carefully lest they lose their footing and plunge downward to certain peril. The Bishop's footfalls were slow and methodical. He had little doubt that the prisoner behind each door would be frightened, wondering at the sound and that their own door would suddenly open. Each man had prepared for his own execution, but in truth it was not execution that delivered the most souls, it was despair and loneliness, for under such conditions even the strongest soul is destroyed. Cold, darkness, bitter loneliness, hunger and isolation were the tools of despair and it took a strong man to wield such instruments and not fall beneath the weight of such a load.

Jacob inserted the key and turned until he heard a loud click. Then he opened the iron door and entered into the second level of security. This small space was also like a cage, a cage within another cage. Following Stephan's instructions, he closed the outer door and then turned back to face the second door. The second door had a smaller door with a shutter for which the keeper could see through and speak with the prisoner. At the bottom of the door was another compartment for passing food and collecting waste. Jacob was revolted at the thought of living under the crushing burden of such conditions, and even though he knew that the prisoners deserved the punishment given to them, his revulsion was no less acute, no less visceral. He took a deep breath and said a quick prayer. Then he slid the shutter open.

Inside the cell was dark; only a dull beam of light penetrated in from a single, barred window almost ten feet above the floor, so that the prisoner could never look out into the world again. Jacob looked deeper into the cell. In the corner, partially lost in shadow, was a stone slab, covered with coarse, woolen blankets. Laying on the slab was the form of a man. Jacob could not tell if the man was sleeping because he faced the wall and was almost completely hidden from the light. He could have been dead. Jacob waited a few moments to see if he would move, and when he did not, he called out to him.

"Barabbas, are you awake? My name is Bishop Jacob, and I have come to speak with you."

No sound came from the heap, but Jacob saw it move and he knew that Barabbas had heard him. He called again.

"Barabbas, rise and speak to me. I have not come to harm you." Then he took a tomato from his pocket and held it through the bars. "I have brought you something to eat," he said. "Take it Barabbas and eat it, for I know that you are hungry."

"Can you open the inner door?" came the weak voice of Barabbas.

"No, I cannot open that door," Jacob replied. "Only the Keeper can open that door. But in truth, I would not open that door even if I could, for you are charged with sorcery, Barabbas."

"Then go away and leave me to die," Barabbas snarled. "For what purpose do you come to me now? Would you presume to bring comfort to a sorcerer?"

"My purpose is to bring comfort to the soul," Jacob countered with conviction. "And though you have been cast away the Lord still loves you, for your soul is part of the Lord, Barabbas."

Barabbas remained still. He said not a word.

"Are you listening to me, Barabbas?"

"Words!" Barabbas spat. "Words, words, and more words. My life has been reduced to words spoken by men of words. I am sick of it!"

Bishop Jacob frowned noticeably. "That is not true," he said. "Through deeds we are able to prove . . ."

"Words!"

"I see that suffering sharpens the tongue, does it not, Barabbas?"

Barabbas spoke out with disgust. "What do you know about suffering?" and he raised his head in defiance and looked into Jacob's eyes. "To you, suffering is just more words . . . stories! The suffering of the Lord is not your suffering, Bishop."

The Bishop looked away and averted the terrible eyes of Barabbas. A feeling not unlike the bitterness of guilt started to form in his mind, but only for a moment. Then the Bishop fired back.

"All suffering is for the Lord," he declared. "I could talk to you about St. Dominic . . ."

"Words!" Barabbas shouted furiously. "Why do you come here but for to torment me? You do not know me, Bishop. Have you even seen my face? You have not, and yet you speak to me about suffering as though you were suffering."

"Come Barabbas," said Jacob without reproach. "Take this and eat it, for your hunger must be great."

And then Barabbas moved into the partial light and Jacob saw that the once mighty man was now wasted and weak and his movements were slow and strained. The man described to him by King Sigmus was gone, and now only a fragment of that man remained.

"Once I cast down a lamb into the eternal abyss," said Barabbas rising painfully to his feet. "Once I was a man of great strength, and man of deeds. Look at me now."

Black, oily, mangy hair fell about his weary face and he had not the strength to push it back. He faced the Bishop and he was pathetic to see. The look in his eyes was empty, devoid of thought, devoid of intelligence, and not unlike the eyes of a reptile. Barabbas stood up with great difficulty. Then he walked a few paces to the door and gently took the tomato from the outstretched hand of the Bishop, and Jacob saw that his hand trembled. Jacob watched uncomfortably as Barabbas caressed the tomato and held it like a newborn chick. His heart was moved by what he saw.

"Have you had dealings with the devil, Barabbas? Have you sold your soul? I can only help you if you speak the truth."

Barabbas stopped eating. He raised his head and met the eyes of the Bishop with anger. Jacob thought that Barabbas would throw the tomato at him, but he did not. Shaking his head side to side slowly, he said.

"No, I did not do what I have been accused of doing. I have been wrongly accused."

"All men that are condemned say that they are innocent, Barabbas. I know this King, he is a good man, and I do not believe that he would lie to me. Tell me why I should believe the word of a condemned sorcerer over that of a King, Barabbas."

Barabbas took a step back. Then he fell to his knees in supplication.

"I am begging you," he said. "Listen to what I have to say, and then judge for yourself."

"How can I believe you if you are what the King tells me you are?"

"You will know," was all that Barabbas said. Then he began to tell the Bishop a very different story than the story the King had told.

"I was a good man, a man of God. My family I took care of and I tended my sheep and kept them safe from harm. Yes, my life was a life of service, service to my sheep, service to my family, my wife, and service to my God. But such service only makes a man greater but for his toil, and I toiled happily and without distraction. But the devil watches us and the devil waits for us to tire from our toil, and that is when the devil strikes, for in our own weakness the devil finds strength.

"One day, one of my sheep wandered too close to the precipice. There are treacherous falls on the mountain it is true, and I would have tried to save it but I was too far away. Instead, my young boy tried to rescue the mislaid sheep for I had taught him to love his work and to protect those within his charge. And there I watched as my precious boy fell over the precipice and plunged onto the rocks below. My heart nearly failed me in that moment, but it has been my good fortune to be healthy and strong . . . ah, would that only I had died on that terrible day instead of my young boy, and yet it was my terrible fate that I would live to see an even more bitter misfortune unfold.

"Sometimes it is a bitter fate to be born strong, for myself that is true, but for my tender and fragile wife that was not her fate. Her heart was pure, that is true, but her heart could be easily broken. Yes, her weakness, beautiful though it was, brought her to her knees and destroyed her. In an act of utter despair, she cast herself over the precipice, into the abyss, and into hell.

"Does one ever recover from such woe? What terrible fate to suffer endlessly the bitter torment of such loss. To die would be a welcome mitigation from such anguish, but it was my terrible fate to be strong and to survive. Yes, I tried to take my own life, but I was too weak, for I imagined that the Lord needed me and that the Lord had other plans for me. And so I prayed. Never were prayers uttered with more compassion or through more tears than the prayers that I prayed ceaselessly during that dreadful period. But the Lord did not hear me and my prayers evaporated.

"So I prayed to the saints, for I was convinced that if my prayers were pure enough that the saints would intercede on my behalf. Oh, how I prayed! Oh, how my heart swelled with hope and with contrition for the love and for the compassion of the saints, oh, how strong I was in this righteous endeavor.

"Every night I prayed. Every night I lit candles and prayer lamps to keep my

resolution strong and to not lose faith in my desire, for it was my desire that my wife should be forgiven and I had no thought for myself.

"And so one night as I prayed for intercession I was attacked. I stood in the center of my humble cottage and I tore my heart out that my tiny voice might be heard above the vast cry of the multitude. That is when the door of my cottage was broken down with such furious violence that I was frightened that the Lord had come to strike me dead. But it was not the Lord that battered my door in that fateful night . . . it was the King, King Sigmus. His eyes were terrible in their fury and he attacked me without mercy. I tried to fight back, I tried to make him stop, but he was too strong and with powerful blows he beat me into submission. When I recovered my senses, I was where you see me now."

"How dare you bring such false witness against the King?" Bishop Jacob said through his disbelief. "How dare you?"

Barabbas saw the expression on the face of the Bishop and he knew that his cause was lost. With a sigh of acceptance he turned his back upon the Bishop and stumbled to his bed of rags. Then he sat down and his head fell lifelessly upon his chest. Beckoning calls from the Bishop remained unanswered until the Bishop finally closed the latch and went away. When the Bishop was gone Barabbas shuddered, and the devil came out of his body.

The Children

Round and round the passage scaled the ponderous structure built long ago as a watchtower. Permanently damp and dank, the shifting stone had cracked over the centuries and like a rotting skeleton, poisoned the very air within. Jacob walked a few paces behind the King and he followed the gentle swishing and swaying of his long cloak as it disappeared around a bend. The bleakness being almost complete, Jacob suddenly remembered the innocent children of his parish, and inexplicably a smile came over his face.

Bishop Jacob walked along the coastal footpath between Kirk Michael and Bishopscourt so that he could look out to sea and meditate, and often his thoughts drifted all the way to the Emerald Island, enchanted, eternal, the island of the saints. The wind from the sea was steady and strong and his coat whipped about like sailcloth as he gathered it around him. Standing so high above the roiling sea he felt small, and though he be a bishop in the larger world, on the island he was small and the purpose of his life but to serve the Lord. The sky was overcast and a white haziness obscured the view along the coastline as far as Peel Harbor. So beautiful it was along the precipice, so beautiful was God's work, the stony, windswept grasses and yellow gorse filled him with joy, and it was the isolation, the absence of conflict, the very loneliness of this place that gave him the greatest comfort. But for the sound of sea birds and wind he would hear his own thoughts like whispered words. Against the crumbling ruins of an old cottage Jacob sat down facing the sea and gathered the folds of his coat around him, and laying his head back, closed his eyes and drifted into the sublime world of his thoughts. When he opened his eyes again he felt refreshed and renewed, and he walked back to Bishopscourt full of hope.

Like Christ the Shepherd, the duties of a bishop are to shepherd the mystical body of the Church as one of Christ's apostles and to teach by example the lessons of which Christ became incarnate in spirit. The bishop is called to bear witness to the spirit of the Lord and to be a light in the darkness of ignorance and despair. The bishop leads his people, and by the grace of the Lord guides them in righteousness and faith. But as an emissary of Christ, an envoy of the Church, the bishop must be on guard against the lies and treachery of the devil, and the bishop must be strong at all times. And when Bishop Jacob began to weaken from the load, he consigned himself to prayer until the strength of the Lord returned and filled him with glory. And so Jacob prayed until the weakness of doubt was replaced with the fire of certainty, and then out into his parish he went once again to administer to his flock.

Bishop Jacob wandered the paths and byways of his parish and the people came to him and gathered around him because they knew him by his walk, his slow, solitary graceful stride that informed them of his great ruminations and they wanted to be near him. He spoke the wisdom of the Lord, but often he merely listened to the troubles of his people and he felt his heart swell when they were uneasy and in pain. The children gathered around him and knew nothing of his great compassion. The children sensed in the Bishop something special, something that was unspoken, or perhaps it was something not entirely defined in the Bishop yet, but something that he only was destined to achieve, something that was to be. They would gather around him and hold hands, and they would dance in circles around him for they loved him so. The Bishop drew vitality from their presence like an ephemeral hummingbird sucking sweet nectar from a precious flower, and a smile from the Bishop would fortify the children in their playfulness.

One day Jacob was stopped to talk with a group of children that had gathered around him. The children laughed as they danced around him and their song was sweet and their sing-song voices beautiful. The smallest of the children, a girl of eight or nine years named Maria, pulled at the Bishop's cloak and smiled so tenderly that the Bishop was moved to tears, for never having children of his own he could only imagine the joy such a gift from God could bring. Maria had shiny black hair and tiny pigtails and her smile, so wide and bright, was far away and strangely melancholy. Jacob smiled, for he loved the children, their innocence, their fearless capacity to love, and he thanked the Lord for the joy they could bring.

"Alright," Jacob said with a laugh as he gently pushed them away. "Stay back now and let me see if I have anything for you."

Then he searched in the folds of his cloak and brought out a piece of sugar candy, and breaking it into small pieces gave some to all the children. The children laughed and held out their tiny hands. When all the children had a piece of candy Jacob smiled and said.

"Are you happy now?"

The children clapped their hands and begged to hear a story. They knew that Bishop Jacob knew many stories, and that he was fond of telling them.

"Alright now," he said, and he raised his eyebrow. "Would anyone like to hear the story of the bird that sang only at night?"

The children laughed and sat down in a circle around the Bishop. Their faces were dirty, but their smiles made them look like tiny angels.

"Once there was a bird," the Bishop began, "that would only sing at night when it was dark and all the other birds had gone to sleep. Now some birds, it is true, liked to work during the darkest hours, but their song was harsh, and their song was frightening, and their song was doleful. The bird that sang at night was different, for this was a very special bird and it was completely purple, except for a crown of white that covered its head. It was very easy to see during the daylight hours, but at night it was almost invisible.

"Now many songbirds like to sing during the daylight hours and their joy is also the joy of all those that are near and can hear its sweet song. The world is filled with the joy of song for that is the way the Lord has made it.

"But one day the bird that sang at night spoke to the Lord, for the Lord knows the language of all creatures, and pleaded to be allowed to sing at night. Now the Lord inquired of the little bird that it might tell Him why it should like to sing at night when the other songbirds were sleeping. The bird said that it was so that it might bring hope to all the myriad creatures that are frightened and hunted and too terrified to sleep, and that they may be comforted. The Lord inquired how the innocent bird knew of such things as terror and prowling, lurking, hunting creatures that inhabited the darkest hours. The little bird said that it had been told of these things by a wise magpie. Now the Lord knew the terrible treachery of the magpie but said nothing to the bird about it. Instead, the Lord allowed the bird to have what it wanted, but only with one condition. The Lord instructed only that the bird should never try to warn the creatures of the night, but only that its song should bring them peace and solitude. The bird at once agreed, for it did not know the reason for all things under the sun and some things are better left unknown.

"And so the bird that sang only at night filled the forests and glens with sweet music and the silent creatures were comforted. But when the magpie heard of this it was furious. The magpie went around to all the creatures of the forest and whispered into their ear that the bird that sang at night was harmless and that it could be easily devoured. Then the magpie told them that to eat the innocent bird would satisfy them and they should never want for food. And so the creatures of the night began to hunt the bird that sang only at night and the poor bird was almost captured many times. The bird that sang only at night knew of its own terrible danger, but still it did not cease its beautiful song at night because it had promised the Lord to be faithful.

"And so it was that the Lord saw what His own tiny creature was doing, and the Lord was pleased. That is when the Lord decided to make the bird that sang only at night invisible to all the creatures of the night so that it would always be safe. And that is when the Lord granted the bird that sang only at night eternal life so that its song should never perish from this Earth. And if you listen carefully sometimes when you are woken during the night, you can sometimes hear the sweet song of the Lord's special bird, the bird that sang only at night."

The children erupted into laughter when the Bishop finished speaking. They stood up and began dancing around him and they started to sing. So overcome with joy was the Bishop that suddenly his feet took flight, and to the laughter and singing of the children, the Bishop rose into the air and floated above their heads and like a gently listing ship, and with his arms and legs spread apart like wings, levitated over them in joyful bliss.

Cristen Meets the Devil

"Some men must be forever lost," King Sigmus turned his head and spoke to the Bishop who was following close behind in shadow. The sound of his voice was hollow and was swallowed by the emptiness. "For even as the Lord wrought destruction upon the people, so we must condemn certain people that the entire population not succumb to temptation and be thus destroyed."

"And yet the Lord often entertained the company of sinners, Sigmus. The righteous have no need of salvation, but the sinners must perish without hope. In truth, it is such that the sinners have more need of Christ than do the righteous."

Just outside of Castletown, and passing through the narrow streets past old fishing cottages, shops and taverns, one comes to an inn called *The Blacksmith*. Lonely fishermen, sea hags, scoundrels, wandering woodchoppers, tramps and sinners, all come for cheap food and drinks and to hear the latest scandals and for tales of witchcraft, witchery, werewolves, and distant wars. The darkness that permeates the inn hides much and the tap-master is none too particular about what happens in the darker corners. Good folk don't beat its door down to get in, but the tap-master doesn't care. What the good folk don't see never happened and never was, no one knows and no one cares to know. What happens inside is good . . . for all the better it doesn't happen outside.

The devil, sitting at a table in a dark corner lit only with a single candle and crushed beneath clouds of heavy smoke, sipped craftily on a glass of ale. Across the table sat another man, a poor wretch who had been driven to drink by the loss of his only child. The man knew not with whom he drank, but even the company of a devil is preferable to being alone to some men. He would drink until he could no longer feel the pain, and then he would crawl home and fall into the arms of his unreceptive wife who had run out of tears.

"We must raise a glass together," said the devil, who went by the name of Shem. "Let us make a pact," he said again with a smile. Then he raised his glass. "To the abyss," he said cleverly, downing his drink and slamming the empty glass on the table with a thud.

"To the abyss," the man agreed passively and finished his drink.

The devil promptly ordered more drinks, becoming loose with his money and buying drinks for all his new friends. Yes, the devil made friends wherever he went. Then he leaned in close to his new friend and whispered in his ear.

"Cheer up my friend, you only live once. To the devil with the future. The future is now."

"I feel sickened by it all," said the man who was called Cristen. "I don't deserve to live, and I don't want to if only I could have my boy back. Alas, oh why did the Lord have to call him home so young?'

"Perhaps the Lord is punishing you," the devil suggested. "Are you a sinner, my friend?"

"A terrible sinner," he answered weakly, for the acknowledgment of his own sin revolted even himself. And now he was close to tears again. "I cannot stop. No, I cannot and I sin every day and every hour and every second of my life, for my life is sin. Indeed, my life . . ."

The devil laughed. He was thoroughly amused. Then the devil took a long pull from his glass and said.

"Don't you understand that to sin is to exist? Sin brings us to life, my friend. Sin allows us to feel, and to think! Without sin you would surely fade away like smoke for you would have no purpose. Do not be ashamed of your tears brother. Do not be ashamed to feel . . . and to love. Ah, but the Lord would have us love only the Lord. I prefer . . ."

"You are a great sinner as well," said Cristen through watery eyes. "Together we should but perish with shame."

The devil was offended. "No, no, no my friend, do not be ashamed. Do not fear what you do not understand, and do not fear evil. Evil is good. Evil is here to help us live in a world without love. Come now, finish your drink."

Cristen was very drunk and now his thoughts were true. The slurred words came through his swollen face and puffy eyes as he tried to see the face of his friend which kept changing.

"Love is evil," he moaned. "Never love," he said parenthetically.

The devil agreed. "False love is evil, yes. But to protect the love that is within us is beautiful," he continued. "The vile, sickening creatures that would try to seek love from us is what we must fight, for they plead with us and beg us for our love, and like vampires they suck from us our vital essence until we are weakened."

"Indeed, love makes us sick," Cristen agreed.

The devil continued to buy more and more drinks until Cristen could barely keep his eyes open and rubbed them with difficulty. Cristen had lost track of time. He wanted only to sleep. Now the devil was satisfied. He looked around at the gloomy haze that hung inside the room, and the voices, disembodied by the smoky darkness, seemed to come from another world. The devil smiled and said that it was time to leave and he escorted Cristen out into the night air.

"Let us walk together," the devil said as he gently took hold of Cristen's hand and led him along.

They walked together for a long time until Cristen became disoriented, seemingly walking in his sleep. When the devil stopped they were standing on a high cliff overlooking the sea. The night was dark, but the moonlight shone brightly on the silver waves. Cristen slowly regained his senses even as the devil was already speaking to him, but Cristen could remember nothing.

"Now is your chance to find love," the devil was saying. "Do you have the courage to fulfill your promise?"

Cristen shuddered. "What promise?" he asked. "I remember no promise."

"If you give me what I ask," the devil insisted, "then I will give you what you ask in return. You can believe me when I say that I have made many bargains"

"And what do you want?" Cristen asked.

"Your life!" the devil announced triumphantly, and suddenly he began to glow as a silver outline of light enveloped him like a halo. "Behold the Morningstar," he said. Then the body of the devil fell away like the dead skin of a snake and a radiant being of utmost beauty stood before Cristen like an angel. "The Lord cannot abide your sin," the devil said. "But I find it beautiful. Worship me and you shall live for eternity, in sin, in separation, in love. Obey me now and you shall suffer never again for your sin."

Cristen tried to speak but his fear was so great and his trembling so profound that he could not move and even his mind became petrified. Face to face with such awesome power, he felt weak and insignificant. He tried to pray but the words of the prayer were choking him, causing greater and greater fear. Finally the broken man fell to his knees and raised his eyes to the sky in silent supplication, pleading for help. The devil, seeing that he would not get what he wanted, became angry. He pointed down at the cowering man and proclaimed.

"You will worship me!"

Cowering, demoralized and completely drained of will, Cristen started to shake violently.

"Worship me or die!" the devil shouted with authority.

Cristen twisted and writhed on the ground before the majestic angel of light, frightened and revolted. His fear was so great that once his decision had been made, his determination to see it fulfilled overpowered his inability to move and he was suddenly propelled forward, past the angel of light, and threw himself headlong over the precipice.

The Wasteland

Bishop Jacob felt his stomach lurch and he became aware of his hunger. He had not eaten that day and his hunger only made him more acutely aware of the hunger of all men and the hunger of the Lord, for the Lord would that no man should perish from the hunger of the spirit.

King Sigmus took breakfast as usual in his private chamber. Iona came in carrying the breakfast tray: eggs, toast, ham, blueberry jam, juice, and tea. In a small antechamber she arranged the dishes and cups and flatware. On the table was a crystal vase out of which a folded paper rose decorated the simple setting. When everything was arranged she called:

"Sigmus. Sigmus, come my dear. Breakfast is served."

The King entered from another antechamber. He was carefully adjusting the fit of his brightly colored waistcoat.

"Ah, thank you Iona. This looks wonderful as usual, and you have caught me in a hungry mood. Yes, I am famished, that is true." Then he smiled at her and winked.

Iona smiled back at the King. "I felt the presence of a ghost in my room last night," she quipped. "It followed me to my bed."

"That was only I," said Sigmus with a laugh. "Even ghosts can get cold during the night, but I can see that we are both safe now."

Iona smiled and kissed the King fearlessly. Then she took a seat.

"Yes, sit my dear. Let us eat and I will tell you something interesting."

Iona held out her cup and the King poured her tea. She brought the cup to her mouth and sipped like a little bird, for she was very pretty and the King loved to watch her delicate movements. They ate their breakfast with relish. The early morning was their time to be alone without a breach of protocol and questioning eyes and they enjoyed this time and were happy. Then the King wiped his mouth and reached for his tea.

"There are strange happenings throughout the land, Iona."

Iona smiled, for the King often prefaced one of his stories with similar statements, and then the King would wind a long and often incongruous story. Now his joy was also her joy and she listened to each story and tried to guess what he was talking about, for she had come to know and love his obfuscations.

Sigmus returned her smile. "No Iona, this is not a story. I am quite serious this time. Then he told her of the many varied and ephemeral encounters with angelic beings that seemed to descend from heaven, only to take flight soon after speaking sometimes only a single word to a wandering Manxman or Manxwoman digging potatoes in the field. Iona was astonished.

"What does all this mean, Sigmus?"

"I do not know," he answered truthfully. "If indeed we are being visited by messengers, I would like to know why, but if these visitations be the work of evil, then I must prepare to fight it. I am going away for a while, Iona. You will be safe here, I promise, and I will not have to worry about you."

Later that afternoon King Sigmus rode out of Ballasalla and galloped over the Crosshag Bridge on his way to Castletown. In the heart of Castletown, between the Castle Brewery and the George Inn on Arbory Street, is a smaller inn called The Globe, clean and well-lit, which is renowned for its spicy rum and smoked herring. There he met with some of his local deemsters and was briefed on several occurrences he was not hitherto aware of, occurrences he would agree that were better left unknown.

Padeen Williamson stood up even before the King had taken a seat. The man was short, stout and loud. He shouted.

"There can be no doubt about it . . . the devil has come to Man!"

Several voices rose up in a cacophony of noise and would have driven the proceedings into chaos but for the power and authority of Gorry Hansen, a local Deemster and noted expert on the occult and occultist lore. When he stood up tall like a strapping oak tree, and raised his arm defiantly, the shouting stopped.

"*King Sigmus*," he announced forcefully but with deference.

Everyone stood up at once. Gorry Hansen, a tall, elegant man dressed in formal black tail-coat and elegant black pointed shoes was not the least bit concerned by the almost hysterical actions of the other men present, and it was a tribute to his intelligence that those present deferred to *him* when it came to summing up the present situation for the King. He motioned for everyone to be seated, and then he explained.

"Notwithstanding the instances of supernatural sightings you no doubt have already been made aware of, several other . . . rather curious deaths have been reported, all in the course of a fortnight. The most recent death was reported as a suicide, but upon investigation, our assessment has been amended."

King Sigmus wrinkled his nose thoughtfully. "Amended? Please explain what you mean when you say amended."

Nervous laughter broke out in the chamber; chairs were creaking beneath the weight of twisting, squirming, shifting bodies of uncomfortable men. Sigmus saw the obvious apprehension and he knew that there was much more to learn. He waited patiently, but secretly he was also becoming apprehensive. Hansen looked at the men and scowled, and the stirring subsided.

"We found the smashed and broken body of Michael Kennaugh on the rocks beneath Bradda Head, Port Erin. It was obvious that he had either jumped or had fallen. But when we went to the top of Bradda Head, we were met with an even more frightening image. In part, we found another body . . ."

"In part?" Sigmus spoke up suddenly.

Gorry Hansen inclined his head slightly toward the King. "Perhaps I may have used the word *body*, too lightly," he said. "What we found was not exactly a body. What we found was more like a shell . . . the skin."

Sigmus gasped. "Oh, my God. Someone skinned him alive?"

"I wish that had been the case," Hansen said sullenly. "If that was the case we would have an explanation, but in truth it is much worse. The skin was intact, Sigmus. The entire body was intact . . . except that it was shriveled away, drained, and completely empty of substance. We found no flesh, no bones, and no organs. We found nothing but a layer of skin, an identity."

"Like the skin of a snake!" Padeen Williamson added. "Yes, this is exactly like the skin of a snake, and it is my belief that no man, though he be Christian or pagan, ever lived inside of it. And just as a snake sheds its skin, so too the devil has shed his skin."

Sigmus turned to face Williamson. The man looked to be eternally frightened.

But Hansen was unconvinced.

"More like a parasite," he said. "For what is it that can devour a man from the inside?"

King Sigmus and the Deemster Hansen spent the next two days traveling to the places on the island where the most remarkable stories were told of strange sightings: creatures rising up into the air only to vanish again without a trace, conversations with angels, demons, ghosts and a myriad of hellish shadows and miasmas. They discovered that places most often associated with strange occurrences often were places of Christian burials and sites dedicated to the saints. Sadly, most of the contacts ended tragically, and murders, suicides, robbery, molestations and necromancy prevailed. When the King returned to his castle, he was convinced that the people were right to be frightened, for indeed the devil had come to Man.

The Anchorite

King Sigmus stopped in front of an iron door and waited for the Bishop to catch up. Below, the faint footfalls of the Bishop sounded like the faint scratching of rats through hollow walls. The Bishop was slow to ascend and the King waited to see his shadow against the stone before he pointed to the door.

"This man robbed his neighbor while they slept," he said. "They caught him stealing their nets. The Lord also cast nets, did He not? Is this man worthy of mercy, Jacob? Do you have mercy on sinners, but not upon righteous men?"

"The Lord cast His nets far and wide, Sigmus. This man will die here," Jacob replied timidly.

"Yes," Sigmus answered. "God willing."

Bishop Jacob knew nothing of the King's investigations, but now he too was searching for clues to explain the strange sightings. He was convinced that the story of Barabbas was connected, and that when he solved the mystery of the one, it would point to the other. Jacob's faith was strong and he believed that the Lord would lead him where he needed to go, so he started walking.

The further north he walked within his parish the less densely became the population until he was in the most remote corner where not a living person presently lived.

The Bishop followed a stony path leading down to the sea. He knew that someone lived nearby because the path was beaten down by the soft trampling of feet. The way was steep and dangerous as loose stones gave way beneath his cautious stride. Down the path he continued to go, looking from one side to the other lest he be surprised and lose his footing. Tightly against the descending slope he knew that ascetic monks had been known to live inside of small caves worn into the cliff. And then he saw him ahead, solitary, and stoic, a man forgotten by other men and by the sweep of time. The Bishop slowed down and approached the man warily.

"Welcome," Jacob said gently. "Peace be with you."

"There is no need to welcome me," the man responded, "for I call no place my home. It would be more appropriate for that I should welcome you, but I welcome no man."

"If that is your wish, then I have no business with you," Jacob said. "But tell me, have you seen a strange man wandering nearby?"

"All men are strange to me," the man answered. "All men are wanderers, for the world is a desert."

"Are you an [6]Eremite then?" Jacob asked.

"My patience with men and with the world of men is short," he answered. "I have no need of these things."

Jacob respected men that were called to the hermetic or ascetic life, men such as Saint Simeon Stylites the pillar dweller, who lived alone atop a sixty foot pillar in the desert, never descending again to earth until his death, but he knew that such forms of extreme living often could displease the Lord, who demanded that men live together in brotherhood. And in the most extreme conditions, desert hermits were often attacked by demons and demonic creatures sent by Satan to bite and to pester and to weaken. He inclined his head slightly to the hermit.

"All men need brotherhood," he said. "Can a man live like a stone and not be broken by the elements?"

"You are a man of God. It is your purpose to bring men to God, but I tell you that my purpose is not your purpose, for I find God in places where other men are afraid to go."

Jacob looked at the lean, emaciated hermit clothed only in sackcloth, and he was astounded. "How long have you been here?" he asked. "I have heard of desert monks living alone, wandering the desert for forty years, eating locusts and scorpions and other vile creatures. Are you one of these men?"

"I am like no other man," the hermit said. "Men of the world would listen to the words of the devil and imagine that those words were from God, but I believe that all the words of man are from the devil. Instead, I listen to the sound of creeping insects and hear the voice of God."

"Yes, I have heard of men like you," Jacob said without contempt. "I have heard that there are men who believe that the world is evil and that the world of matter is evil. Men such as this deny the world of matter and seek only the

---

[6] Eremite: A monk living alone for religious reasons. Not to be confused with an Anchorite, which is a hermit living alone and attached to an Anchorage or holy place.

world of the spirit. But I say that the spirit of God is of the world."

"And yet you live together with other men, squatting, mumbling, and tearing vegetables from the earth. And though I may deny the world of men, there are many men who would deny the world of God because they can hear only the words of the devil."

"The devil corrupts all men," Jacob said unequivocally. "The devil is clever and his ways are wily and secret, but isolation without the brotherhood of other men is dangerous."

"I have seen the devil," the hermit said suddenly.

Bishop Jacob flinched as though he had been stung by the words of the hermit. "Tell me, hermit, what does he look like?"

"The devil looks like all men," the hermit replied.

"Then how can you know that it truly was the devil? How can you know?"

"The devil can be known by his words and by his smile, for the devil smiles while uttering blasphemy and falsehood. In this way you may know the harvest by the taste of a single bite."

"Tell me hermit, what did he say to you? Please tell me for I have been searching for him."

"He tempts me with words," the hermit replied. "The words of the devil can be sweet, and the words of the devil can sound wise to men, but wisdom is in the words of the Lord and all men and their words are like bubbling, babbling filth . . . utter folly! The words of the devil cannot penetrate me for I have been hardened. I say to you that to harden your heart to evil, you must harden your soul."

Jacob's voice became profound in its potency. "I seek the devil, hermit, for I intend to destroy him by the grace of Christ and banish him from the island. Take me to him, if you can."

The hermit looked long and hard at the Bishop until he was satisfied. Then he said, "I cannot take you to him. But if you stay with me for the night perhaps you will see him, for he comes for me at night and he tempts me mercilessly."

"I will do as you say," Jacob replied gratefully. "But time is short now and we must collect wood to build a fire."

"Your faith will keep you warm," the hermit replied. "My name is Anthony and you may stay with me for a night. But we have no need of wood. Better the heat of your own heart than that of the fires of hell."

Then Anthony led the Bishop away. The hermit walked surprisingly confidently across the uneven stones and his footing was sure. Jacob followed carefully and several times had to catch himself lest he fall headlong onto the jagged rocks, for the path was now turned harsh and untended. After a few minutes, the hermit stopped. And then Anthony left the path and crawled up over a hillock. Up against the cliff-face was the darkened entrance of a cave. Outside the cave were the remnants of a few burned logs and a stack of unburned sticks.

"This is where I sleep," Anthony said without pride. "It is fairly simple, but my needs are few and my desires are even fewer."

Bishop Jacob suppressed a laugh for he had no desire to mock the ascetic hermit nor judge the level of his asceticism. "Where do you sleep?" he merely asked for lack of anything better to say.

Anthony opened his arms and cocked his head from side to side. "You're standing on it," he said. "But you may go into the cave if you desire further comfort."

"Do you eat?" Jacob asked, and though he was being quite serious, his words sounded false.

"You are my guest this night," Anthony said, "and therefore we shall break bread together. But in truth I eat very little and most of what I have I give to the birds."

Then Anthony went into the cave and returned several minutes later, arms laden with food and with earthen cups for drinking water. After a prayer was spoken, the two men ate together, and though their fare was humble, only berries and boiled turnips and fish, they were both satisfied, for Bishop Jacob in truth was also remarkably austere. When supper was finished, Anthony arranged a few sticks into a group and lit a small fire.

"Does it get very cold during the night?" Jacob asked, for he wondered how such a frail man could survive beneath such austerity.

"The fire is for us and that we may converse like learned men," Anthony said. "I once was a man of the world and at one time the words of men I studied and made my own."

"And will the fire frighten the devil away?" Jacob implored.

"The fire will draw the devil to us," Anthony responded confidently.

They talked long into the night. They discussed Scripture, for both men were learned, and through their erudition were able to present their belief in elegant form. Jacob knew that much of what he was hearing was apocryphal, forbidden, condemned, and even heretical, but he listened and he defended his Church vociferously. These ideas were not new to him. Jacob knew of many religious sects which questioned Christ's divinity and the Resurrection and the existence of hell and the nature of salvation, and each time he came across vestiges of such heresy he lamented that the Church had not been diligent enough bringing those outside of the Canon back again into the light of truth. And Jacob lamented that so much truth should be lost in the exposition of contrary and dangerous opinions; he also knew that truth needed to be established, and that contrary opinions could be espoused forever in clever forms of thought and words and iconography. But mostly he knew that truth, once established, had to be defended lest the devil infiltrate the Church through the guise of intellectualism.

Sometime during the long night Jacob fell asleep. When he woke, Anthony was looking down at him. There was a strange expression on his haggard face and he studied the Bishop as though he were a specimen of a particular flower that he was trying to identify. With difficulty Bishop Jacob shook off the torpor to which he had fallen, as though he were being held down and had to struggle to wake.

"I must have fallen asleep," he admitted. "Were you saying something?"

"I was saying that you have a beautiful face, and that as you were made in God's image . . . perhaps He looks like you."

Jacob was aghast and he jumped to his feet angrily. "How dare you commit such blasphemy?" he scolded. "It is a very serious sin to think in this way, Anthony. But it is an even greater sin to speak aloud, the blasphemy of such thought."

Anthony smiled broadly. "It is no sin to be born beautiful, Jacob. There is nothing to fear lest you condemn as ugly, the very image of . . ."

"Stop!" Jacob commanded. "Do not say it, Anthony. What has happened to you?"

In a brief moment a sudden change, like a swift sweeping shadow, came over the hermit and he once again regained his composure, becoming as he was before, the quiet and meek ascetic. Jacob saw the transformation and he became very concerned. The hermit became motionless.

"Are you alright?" he asked.

But Anthony was ashamed and could not look the Bishop in the eye. He spoke warily, like a man confessing to a transgression. He spoke and there was pain in his voice.

"Even a few hours of contact with the material world is too much," he said sadly, not daring to lift his head. "Even the slightest contact with matter is too much. Now I have sinned a great sin and I must leave here and go back into the desert to burn myself clean and tear the devil from my flesh."

"Wait!" Jacob cried with compassion. "It is I that should leave. You are already outside of the world of men, Anthony. If you leave here and if you leave now . . . where will you go?"

And then before Anthony could say a word against it, Bishop Jacob took leave and walked out of the cave, into the darkness of the world, into the darkness of his mind. He walked away through the darkness and he regretted his encounter with Anthony, the hermit.

By night, the hills of Man are frightening and local Manxmen do not like to travel alone when creeping monsters and spreading mists and other sorceries are at work. Bishop Jacob however had no such apprehensions, for he was protected by the power of the Lord. All through that long night, the Bishop walked. Across the river Neb and over Slieau Ruy Mountain he walked like a wanderer and his wandering past came back to him with memories of his escape from his frightening guardian. He followed the footpath and fell into a powerful muse. The night sky was clear and he could see without stumbling. His own escape from the world had been one of fear, but it had brought him to Christ and it had showed him the way to his vocation. He seldom brought back to memory those fateful days and he fought them now as they continued to fill his apprehensive mind. He came to a richly forested glen called Dhoon Glen where the trees were thick and images of fairies and wood-devils tried to frighten him, for the folklore of the island was dear to his heart and he did nothing to try to replace it. Then he crossed the Dhoo stream just north of Foxdale and continued until he came to the Silverburn. He followed that until he came to Ballasalla and breathed an exhausted sigh of relief.

When the Bishop arrived at the castle he was told that King Sigmus was not there, and that he and deemster Hansen were traveling together to remote parts of the island. Jacob went away feeling a growing sense of foreboding, but he was powerless to do anything about it until he had a chance to pray and reflect upon the events of the previous night. He decided to stop at Rushen Abbey and speak with the abbot; perhaps he would have more information about the strange occurrences troubling the parish.

After the office of Matins was over Jacob retired to a small cell in the cloister to meditate. It was rare for a bishop to spend much time alone in meditation for his duties were many and his time was short. Bishop Jacob, however, was different. Much of his routine work was given to acolytes and other priests to carry out for as a bishop he could assign his duties in any way he chose and needed answer to no superior to justify his actions. Later that morning, he went to the abbot.

Abbot William looked grave and the lines of his face darkened. "I thought that Manichaeism had been wiped away from the Christian world. Your news causes me great concern, Jacob."

"He is only a simple hermit," Jacob responded. "He is of no consequence. I wanted only to speak to you about his claim to have spoken with the devil."

"With Satan?" Abbot William whispered passionately. "He told you that he spoke with Satan?"

"He used the word devil," Jacob replied. "I am certain that he used that particular word."

William shook his head in despair. "If the devil has come to our shore and has found an ally, there is no limit to the amount of destruction he will deliver upon our people."

"I will ask the Lord for strength," Jacob said. "And I will search until I find this demon . . . and then I will cast it out."

"The devil is in the hermit," Abbot William said thoughtfully. "And though you may cast it out, you will never destroy the will of the devil, for the devil is strong."

The Lamb

Bishop Jacob walked slowly up through the stairwell, and weak, dirty sunlight, filtered in from outside through the narrow key-lights, turned green from incessant sea-spray and droppings from the many birds that circled around and perched in the decaying stone. In a turning, twisting system, the stone passageway coiled to the top like the coiling of a snake, and the further into the tower he ascended the closer to death was his terrible feeling of destiny. Jacob felt like he was crawling up inside the belly of a beast and that the beast was slowly dying even as it devoured him. Behind each door he knew was a man waiting to die, or already dead, and the coldness of the passageway was like the coldness of separation from God. He drew his cloak tightly but there was no warmth.

"Finish your story," said Bishop Jacob to Kerron the Blasphemer. "You have more to tell. I know this. Tell me the reason you were condemned to this prison so that I may know what is in your heart."

Kerron sat on the edge of his pallet and his head hung down limply. "I have suffered," he lamented. "Yes, I have suffered."

"The Lord is not interested in your suffering, Kerron. In truth, the Lord has suffered more than you."

"Has the Lord ever lost one of his children?" Kerron asked with bitterness and rancor, taunting his visitor.

"We are all children of the Lord," replied Jacob with growing frustration. "The Lord cares for His flock."

Then Kerron looked up and his eyes met those of the Bishop. Jacob thought that never before had he saw such blackness, such bleakness, such emptiness . . . such apathy. Kerron's face was wasted and emaciated, and in a final act of submission he finished his story.

"I searched for my child day and night, for what man can sleep when his children are lost and scattered? I walked the streets, the empty paths, the harbors and glens, looking for clues and asking everyone I met if they had seen my child. Sometimes I would fall asleep in trenches and gutters and behind silent buildings only to continue searching when I awoke again. The people stared at me, Bishop. The people looked at me with wonder that I could have so displeased the Lord. Soon they would go into their houses and hide when I would walk past, and in this way I learned pity.

"One day while out searching, I met a man that seemed to know something about my child. He came to me and I knew that he too had been searching. 'Where is she?' I begged him to say.

"He looked at me and I saw pity in his eyes. 'I will take you to her,' he said. 'But do not be hopeful that she still lives.'

"We walked together along the high cliffs north of Peel Harbor in silence and he did not try to comfort me with useless words. Long we walked and I thought only of my child. At last he turned down a path leading down to the sea. About halfway down we went off the path and climbed over a small hillock. And there before us was a small cave cut into the earth . . ."

"A cave?" the Bishop interrupted upon hearing the word.

"Yes," Kerron continued. "He brought me to the entrance of the cave and pointed. "Inside I think you will find your child."

"I ran wildly into the cave. It was very dark inside, but I could see the outline of a man. He looked very old and wore tattered sackcloth like an impoverished monk. 'Where is my child?' I snarled at him.

"He was very calm and his calmness made me quake with fear. 'She is gone,' he calmly said.

'Tell me where she is!' I shouted with rage.

'The devil demands a sacrifice,' he answered. 'I have given her to the devil.'

"I charged him and would have torn him to pieces, but my hands passed right through his body like it was smoke and I watched him disappear. The shimmering image of his body dissipated like smoke . . . like smoke. I looked all around for the man who had led me to the cave, I called, I shouted everywhere, but he too was gone.

"I went back to my home and my anger filled me with purpose. That day I felled two trees and stripped them and planed them until they were suitable for my purpose. Next I tied the pieces together to form a cross. Then I went out into the pasture and searched my flock until I found a young lamb. I led the lamb back to my house where I laid it on the ground before me. My anger had turned to strength. I took hold of the innocent lamb and tore its front legs from the sockets brutally while trying to block out the terrible bleating and baying of the struggling lamb. Then I held each leg over the crossbeam, and with deliberate, powerful hammer-falls, I drove a large nail through each leg, pinning the dying lamb to the cross . . ."

"Oh, my God," Jacob cried.

"There is more," said Kerron.

"I do not want to hear it," said the Bishop. "You have committed an act of evil that cannot be forgiven, Kerron. You have committed an act of blasphemy that I wish I had never heard. You will surely be punished for this, Kerron. Yes, you will be punished."

The Wanderer

In truth, the Bishop hated the dreaded prison and every time he visited it a part of him died along with the unfortunate souls which were consumed within, consumed with an unquenchable, overwhelming fire. In truth, the Bishop would that the dreaded prison should sink into the sea and be gone. The Bishop knew that punishment was necessary, for to allow acts of wickedness to go unpunished was itself an act of punishment for the victims of such wickedness. Some men were destined to live apart from their fellow men, living without love, living without compassion. To the Bishop, the prison was a house of horrors filled with such utter wickedness and shamelessness that he sometimes wondered that he should waste even a single moment on such vile creatures as were captured inside. And then he would remember that the heart of man was transient, but the soul belonged to God and his hopefulness would be restored.

Jacob woke from a fitful sleep, weary, exhausted, and restless; but in the restlessness of his sleep came the will and the determination to do what his heart called him to do. He had no right to sleep when his people were so frightened and his parish so vulnerable to forces demonic and fierce. It comforted him to know that the *hours* would always be kept and that the night office of *Compline* was being celebrated now. God willing, the *hours* would be eternal.

The Bishop put his bare feet on the floor and felt the prickling coldness with satisfaction. Bowing his head, he folded his hands and prayed. When his prayer was finished, after lighting a candle, he stood up to get dressed, but he did not don his vestments this day. No, his decision had already been made even before getting out of bed. Instead, he retrieved a chest that was placed in the corner and opened it. He had not opened this chest in many years and the sound of the rusting hinges, the stale odor of frankincense, and the touch of the polished wood filled his mind and shook his memory to the contents stored within. Inside, among other personal effects, was a coarse, woolen cloak, bleached white by the sun, and a staff carved from the sacred wood of a felled oak tree of tremendous size, belonging to Germanic pagans and named [7]Thor's Oak, or the Oak of Jupiter, after being felled by Saint Boniface in the 8th century. These were the vestments when the Bishop had been naught but a wandering peregrine alone in the wilderness, and so they would serve him

---

[7] Thor's Oak. The legend is that when St. Boniface was young he notched a sacred oak tree, venerated and used for sacrificial rites by the pagans, with an axe. After a single stroke, a mighty wind came and blew the tree down. Afterward the angry pagans were converted to Christianity for so great was the God of Boniface. The wood from this tree was used to build a Church dedicated to St. Peter.

again. After speaking briefly with an acolyte, Bishop slipped out into the night and was gone.

If anyone would have seen the Bishop slip out into the night clothed as he was, they would have suspected him to be a robber or a lurking fiend, but only the eyes of a few restless birds and nocturnal creatures would witness the first steps of the Bishop's dark journey.

The Bishop was walking along the seaside cliffs south of Kirk Michael when the sun came up and the first rays of light pierced the thick clouds and fell upon his white cloak. In the distance, Jacob could hear the voices of children. The Bishop turned his head to see a group of children running in his direction, for they had spotted him. Through the thick grass and yellow gorse they came to him with smiles, because even dressed as a wandering monk, the children recognized him. They gathered all around him and laughed at his cloak for they had never seen him so unsuitably adorned. Jacob looked at them all and smiled, but he had nothing to give then this morning. And then he noticed something missing.

"Where is little Maria?" he asked them.

"Maria is sick," they all said. "She cannot play anymore."

"This is sad to hear," Jacob said. "Tell me children, what is wrong with her?"

An older boy named Oshin spoke up. "She has terrible dreams and then she cannot breathe. Her dreams have made her sick, and now she is afraid to come out of her house and her mother watches over her."

"Where does she live?" Jacob asked with concern. "Can you take me to her house?"

So all the children walked along leading Bishop Jacob and he followed them with sadness in his heart and the children were sad because of his sadness. The procession stopped in front of a small, whitewashed house with a thatched roof and a stone chimney. An old woman came out of the house to greet them. She wore a heavy shift that touched the ground and her hair was tied back with a cord. Short, heavy, she was a woman of work and Jacob could see by the crooked way that she walked that her life was one of toil and hard work. But then she smiled.

"Welcome Bishop Jacob," she said unexpectedly.

Jacob nodded. "Good day to you," he said. "Is Maria alright? The children say that she is sick."

The smile suddenly disappeared and the woman's expression turned grave. "She is very sick," she said. "Would you like to see her?"

Maria lay in her bed, and when the Bishop came in, she smiled brightly. The room was dark for the shutters were closed. Jacob looked carefully at her and tried to determine the extent of her illness.

"How are you feeling, Maria?" he asked.

"You look funny," Maria answered. "Are you going away from us?"

"No, Maria," the Bishop answered. "I am merely going for a long walk. But I have come to see you, Maria. Are you feeling unwell today?"

"Sometimes I cannot breathe," she said. "And then I get frightened because I do not want to go away."

The Bishop knelt down on the floor next to Maria and felt her head with his hand. It was warm and damp. "You do not have to go away," he said gently. "What are you talking about, Maria?"

"When I die I am going to be taken to a bad place," she said as her eyes opened wide and Jacob saw her fear.

"You are not going to die, Maria," he said confidently. "What a silly thing for you to say."

"When I cannot breathe," she said anxiously, "a man comes to me in my dreams and tells me that he is waiting . . ."

"No, no, no," the Bishop repeated. Then he touched her face and wiped away a tear. "Do not be afraid," he said. "You must be strong, Maria. The Lord wants you to be strong. I will pray for you and I will speak to the Lord, Maria. Now you stay in bed and get well so that your mother will be comforted. Can you do that, Maria?"

Maria watched the Bishop and took comfort in his words, and though she was truly frightened, she nodded her ascent. Then Bishop Jacob said goodbye.

"I wish that I had known you were sick," he said. "I have no candy for you,

Maria. Bless you, my dear." And then Bishop Jacob left the house and continued on his journey.

The Bishop walked all day and spoke with many people. They came out of their houses and away from their fishing nets to see him and they were anxious to hear all the news of the Lord. Jacob learned that the fishing was good, but that the animals were restless, and that some of them had died. Everywhere he went he was offered food and water to drink for the people were generous with what they had though it was not much. That night the Bishop was offered a room in a small house of a fisherman named Kerrik, a happy Manxman with a good smile and bad teeth. Jacob sat over his supper of herring and lentils and he was thankful. After supper was over, the Bishop and Kerrik sat outside and spoke about matters of importance while Kerrik's good wife cleaned the supper dishes.

"Where are you off to?" Kerrik asked in a friendly manner.

"I'm walking around the island," Jacob answered. "In fact, I'm looking for someone."

"Perhaps I know him," Kerrik responded. "What does he look like?"

"Where this person goes only death and misery follow. Where this person walks, sweep the dust clean of his presence. Like a plague he drags his rotten self across the land and when he is gone the reek of death remains."

Kerrik thought for a moment. "Hum . . . sounds like someone I know. Does he live here?"

"No, he does not live here but travels across the earth like pestilence on the wind. I don't want to frighten you, Kerrik, but I am looking for the devil."

Kerrik leaned back in his chair and sighed. "Haven't seen him," he said. "Devil knows better than to come around my house. We're God fearing you see. You say the devil drives the wind of pestilence, but the Lord drives the wind of the spirit, and the Lord drives the herring and the birds and the beasts, and the Lord drives the rain. Ah, the devil doesn't frighten me . . . it is God that I am afraid of."

The next morning Jacob set out early. He had a breakfast of bread and goat-cheese before leaving. He thanked Kerrik for his hospitality and then he set out walking once again. Jacob breathed the clean air and he was refreshed, for the Lord gave us air to breathe and that it should be good. As far as he could see was goodness. As far as he could see was the vista of land and sea, the meadows of blue and purple sage grass, pale lilac and red bell heather, bluebells, bilberry, the mist shrouded mountains of the interior, the stony paths, everywhere the varicolored wildflowers and the brown, spindly, prickly shrubs and moss that covered the hills like skin; the Bishop saw all this and he was pleased.

The Bishop walked until he reached Jurby Head, where he rested. Then he began walking inland toward Ramsey, but the sun was falling before he reached any suitable dwelling to spend the night and he had to bed down for the night beneath the boughs of an old rowan tree. The Bishop smiled when he remembered the folklore associated with the tree. It was used prominently to ward off evil spirits and demons, so the Bishop laughed when he realized the irony. Twice during the night, however, he was awoken by strange sounds. The first time, he only turned over and fell back to sleep. The second time, he was shaken so violently that he stood up at once and wielded his staff like a fiery sword.

"Who's there?" he called into the darkness.

The wind slipped through the trees lightly and the sound made him focus his discernment and listen more carefully. He could clearly see but a few paces into the trees as the darkness was broken by the passing clouds above. Jacob peered through the darkness in the direction from which the sound came. Then, in the clearing and hovering a few feet off the ground like a mist, he saw a luminous glow. The glow was very dense but also very weak, pulsating and blinking in and out of existence. Jacob stared at the apparition intensely. Now the apparition took shape and coalesced into the form of a man, but still the outline of the shape was tinged with silver light.

"Are you afraid of me?" came a soft voice from the apparition.

Bishop Jacob thrust his staff before him and called: "Are you a man? Show yourself so that I may know you."

And then the glowing apparition coalesced further and descended to the ground. Now a tall, ethereal specter of a man stood before him and waited to be acknowledged.

"Are you Satan?"

"I am," the specter said. "Do you know me by my name?"

"You have no right to be here," Jacob said. "I have not summoned you. Be gone, Satan!"

"Yes, you are beautiful," Satan said. "I admire you for your beauty, but I must hate you as well."

The Bishop felt a numbness crawling up his arm and he could feel the tingling, the prickling of a strange power, a strange authority building within. He looked at *The Great Deceiver* and he felt fear and awe, for he knew that a powerful angel stood before him now.

"May I not go where I am not summoned?" said Satan. "I am free to do as I please," he continued. "It is not I that would destroy his own creation. It is not I that would deny the workings of the body. It is not I that would offer a better world long from now into the future when the world is at hand and the world is beautiful."

"Go away!" Jacob shouted and the surge of power within became stronger.

"The spirit is good," said the devil, "but life is blood. Why do you refuse to live? Why do you deny life? Life must be touched and tasted. Life is in the touch of a woman and the light touch of a breath . . ."

Suddenly the staff of Jacob erupted with a burst of blue flame and would have smote the devil on the spot, but the devil was not there and only a faint, lingering mist dissipated into the night air. The Bishop felt the weakness returning to his body and he knew that the devil would not return. Jacob fell to his knees and thanked the Lord. Then he continued to pray until morning and he was refreshed when the light returned.

In a pouch attached to his belt the Bishop reached in and took out a handful of nuts and berries and so ate a meager breakfast before setting out for Ramsey. When the Bishop arrived he spoke with many people, but he did not speak about his encounter in the forest.

The Norse warrior Godred Crovan, or *Godred the white hand,* known to the Manx as King Orry, invaded the Isle of Man three times. With his army of Norsemen he was defeated by the Manx and forced to flee for his life. A second time he was also defeated and forced to flee. A third time he came with a large army by night and stole into the port called Ramsey, named by the Norse as *Wild Garlic River,* and there he hid 300 men in the nearby wood on the sloping brow of the mountain called [8]Sky Hill. The next day, when the

---

[8] This is the Battle of Skyhill, 1 mile west of Ramsey in 1079

Manxmen gathered for battle, they were ambushed suddenly and driven to the sea by the approaching army where they pleaded for their lives and were spared, and so was the taking of the kingdom from the ruling king, Fingal Godredson, in 1079.

And so, too, had the devil come to Ramsey, stealing through the dark of night, so clever, so powerful and deceitful, intent to ambush the good Manxmen unaware. The devil, however, fought with words and with lies, for he was the king of lies. The devil fought the people with whispered words and with whispered promises and so many Manxmen were deceived.

The Bishop walked vigilantly through the town of Ramsey and his presence drew the attention of many Manxmen not inclined to pass the time with wanderers and men without business; they did not know Bishop Jacob, they did not know that he was there to protect them, and to them he was naught but a reeking vagrant looking for ill-gotten gains. Jacob spoke to a few men hanging around outside of shops, but mostly they shunned him and would not respond to his entreaties. The Bishop walked all day and he looked for signs of evil, but often the presence of evil is vague, unsubstantiated and it is hard to identify; most often the signs of evil only become apparent afterward when the evildoer has escaped, dissipated like vapor and moved on. When the day was over, the Bishop looked for a place to spend the night.

Along the quay on Derby Road, across from the shipbuilding yard, is an old inn called *The Pelican*. The inn had been named long ago when the pelican trouble was at its highest pitch and the town was almost destroyed; and forever more, though the proprietor changed, the name did not. At one time the inn had been the home of an old sea captain named Barnabas, turned pirate, and rumor said he brought the pelicans, which were actually evil spirits, home with him after a long, terrible sea voyage. The pirate was dragged from his home one rainy morning before the children were awake and quartered on the brick outside of his very house, and that is why they say that the color of the brick is forever turned red. This is where the Bishop came to sleep for the night.

Axel Jorgumdson ran the inn with his wife and three daughters. Together they maintained four rooms upstairs and a common room for eating, and the eating was very good if one were in the mood for fish and other creatures dragged from the sea, but the eating was not so good if one were hoping to eat lamb or other creatures of the field. Axel ran the taps and maintained order lest the multitude of fishermen and ship builders and craftsmen start to arguing, which happened every night. Then he would be forced to shout and sometimes fight with the unruly mob, and he wore a faint scar on his face to remind him.

When Bishop Jacob entered the inn Axel scrutinized him for a long time. He had had his share of bad persons with hungry bellies and empty pockets, and he did not particularly like his way of dress either.

"Can you pay?" he asked pointedly.

Jacob nodded. Then he went into the pouch he wore around his belt and took out some coins. He gave one to the proprietor.

"I'm sorry to doubt you," Axel said with a wink. "But I can't be too careful you know . . . especially with the way things are these days."

Jacob nodded again and he wondered what the proprietor meant by his strange words, but he only said. "Can I have a room for the night . . . and supper?"

"Certainly," Axel answered. "Now you go into the dining room and we'll see to your supper," and then he pointed to another room where several men sat around pots of ale and plates of herring and sea scallops.

Jacob went into the dining room which was lit brightly by large candelabras hanging from the rafters above. A few tables were placed in front of the windows which looked out to the harbor. Jacob sat down near the window and soon a young girl came in from the kitchen and went up to his table with a smile. The Bishop ordered his meal and then sat back in his chair and waited. The girl, whose name was Lisha and the youngest daughter of Axel, came back with the Bishop's dinner and asked if he would like anything to drink.

"Bring me a glass of ale," said the Bishop. "It is good for the stomach and it often helps me sleep."

"You will have no trouble sleeping," Lisha said with a smile. "Most folk are afraid to wake up when they sleep in this house."

"Why is that?" Jacob asked, thinking that she was merely trying to amuse him.

"I am only having fun with you," she answered. "I'm sure that you will sleep fine."

After the Bishop's dishes were cleared away he asked to see his room. He was tired from his long walk and wanted only to lay down after his evening prayers and sleep. Lisha told him to go back into the office and that one of the other two girls would take him to his room. The Bishop thanked her and left. At the desk Axel rang the bell and a tall, slender girl came in from an alcove. She was carrying hand-towels.

"Show this gentleman to his room, Myla, would you?"

"Follow me," she said to the Bishop and had to restrain an inclination to laugh for so odd was the Bishop's appearance. Then she went up the stairs and all the way down a passage to a door. Opening the door she waited for the Bishop to enter and then she said. "I will check back with you later, in case you are in need of something."

Jacob thanked her but assured her that he would need nothing. Then he asked her to forget about him and that he would be fine. When the girl was gone Jacob closed the door and went to the bed where he went down on his knees and began to pray.

Sometime during the night he was awoken by a strange sound, like a soft click. He opened his eyes and sat up in bed. All was still and not a sound could he hear from within or without the house. But then he saw a faint glow, a flickering of wan light from a single candle, and in the candlelight he saw his door slowly opening. In a moment it was open and he saw before him a woman holding a tiny candle and the Bishop saw that she was unclothed. Young and beautiful, she was the third daughter of Axel the proprietor, but in her comeliness there was something lurking. Slowly she slipped into his room and stood before him and when she saw that he was awake, she smiled.

"What do you want?" the Bishop asked softly.

She only smiled again and moved closer to the bed where he lay. Her eyes were glassy and glints of light reflecting in them made her seem wraithlike. The Bishop was shocked by her shamelessness; he tried not to notice her nakedness and he wanted to chastise her for her lust, but something stopped him. He could see that she was not fully awake but seemed to be walking as if possessed, dreamlike, trancelike and unaware of her own depravity.

"Come to your senses," the Bishop pleaded as quietly as possible. "Leave my room at once before you are caught."

She smiled again and it was the Bishop's belief that she could not speak and that she was bound by a powerful sorcery. Then she came closer to where he slept and that is when the Bishop leapt out of bed suddenly, though he was unclothed, and took the woman firmly by the arms to restrain her. He shook her violently.

"Come to your senses!" he whispered as forcefully as possible.

Suddenly the woman screamed in terror as the sorcery that held her was broken by the power of the Bishop. She dropped the candle. The Bishop still held her firmly when a man that was sleeping in another room burst into the Bishop's room upon hearing the scream. When he came in he was shocked to find the unexpected nakedness of the Bishop and the woman and he immediately assumed the worst, for he did not know that Jacob was a bishop and a man of God.

"Are you alright?" the man asked, quickly trying to grasp the situation, for he was driven by his desire to protect.

The woman began to cry. Then, as her senses returned completely, she became aware of her nakedness and she tried to cover herself for she was ashamed. Jacob stood there stunned, and in his righteous innocence he was not aware of his own nakedness.

"Are you alright, dear?" the man repeated.

Then Axel stormed into the room and saw what was happening. He carried a candle and, in the light, the horror on his face was visible. Looking first at the Bishop and then to his third daughter, he quickly determined what had happened and he said to the man.

"Go back to bed now, sir. Everything is alright. You have done well, Hans."

Bishop Jacob was sitting on the bed when a soft knock preceded the return of Axel. The proprietor came in quietly and the look on his face was anxious but determined. He stood before Bishop Jacob who was dressed again, and he spoke frankly.

"I do not accuse you of wrong good sir, for I believe that you are true. It was not your fault, and in truth it is the sickness of my daughter that has me upset. She is a good girl and her heart is good."

Jacob looked up with compassion in his eyes. "I have been searching for this thing that can enter the soul, but it has found me instead."

"Are you a man of God?" Axel asked, but he knew that he was in the presence of just such a man.

"I am a sinner," Jacob replied. "Just as all of us are born into sin, I too have been born into sin. The devil is clever, Axel. The devil is clever and he is patient. Silently he moves about, and it is to the weak and the infirm and the uninformed to which he is drawn, but he is after something larger, for it is his desire to wound the Lord. Guard your good house, Axel. Guard your children. I have cast the devil out of this woman, she is safe now, but he may return so be vigilant, be watchful, be prepared and never tire of praising the Lord."

The Devil and the King

King Sigmus ascended the darkened stairwell of the dreaded prison and his heart, too, was darkened by what he must do. Each step brought him closer and with each step his heart became heavier but for his burden. To make the realm safer sometimes a King was forced to do things which his heart was wont to do, but a King, if he be just, buried his emotions for the greater good and though he be troubled his realm was made safe. Yes, the acrid smoke coming from the lamp that he carried reminded him of his duty and his eyes were weary from the bitterness.

King Sigmus went into his private chamber and closed the door. It had been a long day of talking and now he was weary of such talk, but his heart was troubled and he would spend the night again pacing and turning over in his mind the questions which held him fast. In truth, he was worried about his people. As their King he could order that his will be done, but he knew that his will, but for the grace of God, was worthless. And that is why he tormented himself so, for to act without grace was an act of impiety, but it would be his people that would suffer for his failure.

Never had there been such strife, such vulgar lawlessness within his kingdom; never had there been so little reason for strife, for the herring ran steady and there had been no war in generations. But something was happening without provocation and his wisdom told him that evil was incarnate.

Iona was there when he came in. She was waiting patiently for the King to come in because she was worried about him. He was such a good man and she loved him so, but she knew that he took upon himself an impossible burden, for what man could have the answers to all questions? The King smiled when he saw his mistress.

"You are the best thing I have seen all day," he said. And then he kissed her on the mouth and stroked her cheek.

"I have made something for you," she replied, but the King did not hear her, for he was still immersed in thought.

"I cannot understand it," he said. "Why is there such unhappiness? Why do the people live such lives of misery, Iona? Tell me why if you know."

"I am happy," she answered with a smile.

The King held her close and spoke gently. "Of course you are," he said. "You bring me much happiness, Iona, and I thank the Lord for you."

Iona felt safe within the King's powerful arms but she knew that he was battling with something that was pulling him further away. "What is it, Sigmus?" she said. "What is wrong?"

"I have seen death, Iona. I have seen terrible things that I cannot explain. The world is changing and I fear that the apocalypse is at hand, for the door to hell has been opened up upon my land."

Iona tried to bury herself closer to Sigmus. "I'm frightened," she said. "Oh Sigmus, I'm frightened."

Sigmus felt her trembling and his strength returned even as his guilt returned for that he should have tried to share his own fear. He held her firmly and kissed her again. Then he pushed himself away slowly.

"I am sorry to have frightened you," he said, and he caressed her face with love. "It is but my own weakness. Forgive me, Iona. I will discover the source of this new threat and I will meet it. Now, tell me what you have made for me or I fear that you will think that I was not listening to you."

Iona smiled and took Sigmus' hand. "Come with me and I will show you," she said. And she led the King through the inner antechamber to the bedchamber. Thick rugs covered the floor, and though the walls were made of stone, huge colorful tapestries hung and brought warmth, creating an inner atmosphere that was safe and personal.

Laying across the bed was a beautifully woven blanket, for the nights' were long and bitter across the isles. The border was framed within a white, Celtic knot resembling the root system of a tree, comprising an interlocking, interlacing network of braids. But in the center of the blanket was woven a beautiful flower, a single red rose. When the King saw it his eyes watered because he remembered the significance of the wonderful flower. He turned back to Iona and her eyes were watering, too.

"Thank you," he said as his voice began to fail him. "You have made me very happy, Iona."

"It is an endless knot," Iona said. "There is no beginning and there is no end.

The white symbolizes the perfection of Christ."

"As is the love of Christ," Sigmus answered thoughtfully.

During the deepest period of night the King was woken suddenly by a strange presence inside his room. He bolted upright in bed with a jolt. Only the faint sound of the wind rattling his shutters could be heard. A thin beam of moonlight came in through an open window and cast the room in eerie luminescence like strange swamp-light in a sunken glen.

"Who's there?" he called out.

And then, just as he was about to light the candle on his nightstand, he heard another sound and he knew that someone was in his chamber. A thin specter that was the image of Barabbas stepped out of the dark corner from which he watched the King. Silently, the specter stepped further into the chamber until Sigmus saw that it was Barabbas.

"What are you doing out of prison!" he cried.

"Your prison cannot hold me," Barabbas answered. "If I wish to stay, then I will stay, but if I wish to leave you cannot hold me. Unlike you, king, I do not wish to live an ascetic life."

"And yet you have chosen to rot away for an entire year! What do you want with me, Barabbas?"

"I want to know why you are persecuting me," Barabbas answered.

The King lit a candle and started to crawl out of bed. "You are a sorcerer," he said with derision. "I have no need for sorcerers in my kingdom. You have brought the devil to my land, Barabbas, and that is why I locked you away."

"Tell me . . . lord, do you know of men that can occupy two places at the same time? Do you know of men that can fly across the water and pass through solid stone? Do you know of other men that can defy a king?"

"Do not try to trick me, Barabbas. You may prefer to fight with words, but I prefer a sharp sword."

Barabbas laughed. "Will you fight me in your nightshirt? Would you attack me by candlelight?" Then Barabbas waved his hand and the chamber was cast into darkness as even the stars were blotted out. "Do you like the darkness?"

"Darkness for one is darkness for another," the King responded.

Barabbas waved his hand again and the faint twilight returned. "I am the darkness," he said as the candle suddenly flickered to light.

In response, the King threw the candlestick holder at the apparition, but the apparition was gone. The King slept no more that night.

When the sun came up the King rode out to the Bishop's Prison to see if Barabbas was there. The sea was choppy as the boatman carried him across the icy water and he held fast to the side of the boat as it rolled and pitched. Stephan the keeper was there to catch hold of the mooring line and he watched in surprise to see the King, offering him a hand of assistance. The King needed no assistance however, so as soon as he was landed he asked the keeper.

"Has anyone left this prison, Stephan?" the King asked even before stepping out of the boat.

"Neither alive nor dead," Stephan answered as he tried to imagine why the King would ask such a question.

The King ascended the tower quickly until at last he reached the top where Barabbas was kept. Out of breath, King Sigmus waited before opening the door because he did not want the prisoner to see him thus. Finally, he inserted the key and turned until he heard a soft click. Once inside of the inner chamber he closed the door behind him before turning to the inner door. Then, with growing apprehension, he slid back the door panel and peered into the cell.

Barabbas was there. Sigmus had not seen Barabbas since locking him away almost a year ago and he was utterly unprepared for what he saw. Barabbas sat on the edge of the bed within an infusion of foul, grainy light that shone down upon him from a high window as if the very substance of the prison was polluted and poisonous. He sat still, but his body quivered like a gelatinous substance and was more like the substance of a worm or an insect without bone or structure. Barabbas did not know that he was being watched and the King stared with horror, for this was not the man he knew.

Sigmus watched the pathetic man and he had to fight against his impulse for pity because his heart was moved. Yes, Barabbas was a sorcerer, he had been captured by the King and justice had been served, but still he was moved to pity by the sight of such helplessness, such utter collapse. His mind wandered as he watched for he was strangely attracted by the sight and he could not look away. For several minutes he stood in blank fascination until some slight change called his attention to something that was starting to happen.

And like a sleeping animal slowly reviving from a long hibernation or a delicate flower consciously becoming aware of the position of the sun, Barabbas twitched and began to emerge from a deep place of banishment. First it was but a twitch, and like the blood slowly returning to a dormant organ, the life coursed through his body, and as if a skeletal structure now allowed his body to move, his head lifted. Then his eyes opened and, like a monster newly brought to life, he returned to his body. Sigmus was shocked.

"You live," he said softly, for his shock was great. "Do you know me?"

Barabbas stared back at the King but there was no recognition in his weary eyes. Lifeless, thoughtless, without the slightest expression of being, the man could have been dead.

"Look at me," the King continued. "I brought you here, Barabbas. Do you know me?"

With difficulty Barabbas opened his mouth, and like one newly learning to speak, he said. "I do not know you."

Now the King threw his body against the door forcefully. "Do not say that you do not know me!" he shouted. "I was there, do you remember? Are you listening to me, Barabbas?" cried the King, becoming even more angry.

Barabbas only watched the King and wondered at his rage, because in truth his mind was not his own. The devil looked at the King through the eyes of Barabbas and he had to fight against his inclination to smile. No, there would be time for smiles . . . later.

Elias the Denier

Bishop Jacob followed the King closely and he wondered that he should be ascending the tower with such hesitation, such plodding discipline, for surely the King could not be fearful for his own sake.

Bishop Jacob continued to search for the devil and with each village or hamlet that he came to there were stories and rumors and rumors of rumors, for the devil was always one step ahead of him . . . but he was getting closer. In a small hamlet outside of Ramsey a blind man came out to meet him because he heard that a great healer was walking the country. Jacob touched the man's eyes and said a prayer, and no sooner was the man healed and his sight restored. News of the miraculous deeds of the Bishop traveled even faster than he could walk, and at each village would gather the sick and infirm and the Bishop healed many people. People carried food and water out to the Bishop when he passed by and each night he was offered a place to sleep. But the Bishop had not forgotten his mission and he cocked his ear for news of the devil and associates of the devil.

On the sixth day of his wandering the Bishop met with Elias who was later named *Elias the Denier*. So it went that, as the Bishop tramped across the fields of fragrant gorse, the people, curious about the growing legend of the *white monk*, came out to meet him. By this time the Bishop had cast out many demons and had healed many people and the people were convinced that a great saint was at work. The children were the first to reach him and the White Wanderer blessed them all. Next were the women, for the women on the isle were good and they were moved by great passion and great deeds. At last the men came out to meet the Bishop for they would not run before their dreamy wives and exuberant children but that they must show their fierce independence and careful judgment. But in truth it was the men that were the most interested and the most curious, for in the hearts of men great issues burst forth, and though they have no philosophy of their own, they longed for great faith and for great truth.

"We have heard that you have been sent by the Lord," said the leader of the men, and consequently, the man with the most sheep.

"By the grace of God I move with the Lord," Jacob answered.

"We have heard that you seek but to find the devil," the man continued. "Does the devil then walk our land, and how can we be safe?"

"Guard your soul as you guard your flock," said Jacob. "The devil looks for one that is unwary."

Suddenly a tall, thin man with a grey, speckled beard stepped forward and spat.

"I ain't seen no devil," he said curtly. "Been here long enough though. Seen storms to tear the roof off our houses. Seen floods and hail and snow. Seen animals so hungry that they ate themselves, but I ain't seen no devil."

The women gasped and the men frowned and scratched, but the children only gathered around the Bishop and laughed even louder.

"We are all servants of God," Jacob said. "But the devil also has many servants and the devil calls forth his servants for evil. And just as a man may face evil and do nothing, so too is the fate of man if that evil be not met."

"The deeds of a worm are no concern of the Lord, and the deeds of a worm are even less concern to a man than the deeds of the devil, for righteous men are no just soil for the devil."

"Your soul is the soil of the devil," Jacob replied. Then the Bishop looked around and addressed all the people. "Stay vigilant," he said. "The devil may take many forms, and his learning is great. Do not be snared by the trap of his cleverness, but only sigh and invoke the name of Christ."

"Clever words," said Elias the Denier with disgust. "No truer words have ever been spoken, and this is true."

Then Jacob went on his way and the people watched him go and were comforted. But Elias the Denier watched him go and there was bitterness in his heart.

The next village Jacob came to the people were waiting for him. He immediately tended to the sick and prayed for the children. Finally, the village elder stepped forward and addressed the Bishop. The elder was asking for help, for the sea would not give up its bounty.

"This has never happened before," said the elder expectantly. "Each day we go out and each day the breakers turn us back as if the sea were rising against us. We have worked the sea for countless generations and we have paid with the loss of our brave young men. The sea is our life. How can we fight the sea?

How can we ever hope to fight the sea if it turn against us?"

Bishop Jacob listened respectfully. "There are other forces at work here," he said. "There are dark forces at work I fear."

Then Bishop Jacob walked to the edge of the cliff overlooking the sea. The wind whipped his white cloak and lashed his gaunt body, but though the Bishop was gentle, he stood strong as a pillar. The people watched him with anticipation to see what he would do because there were many rumors floating around about the bishop and the people knew the power of words and how words sometimes portended mysterious deeds. Jacob remained quiet for a moment, but then he suddenly held out his hands to the sea and spoke in a soft voice, and slowly the words from his mouth stilled the sea as the calming voice of a father calms a frightened child. One woman fell to her knees and started to pray before the Bishop as if he were the risen savior.

"Rise good woman," Jacob said with authority. "I am not the savior. Go back to your business now and thank the Lord, for the ill wind blows out to sea and a new wind shall bring hope."

Now, when the devil heard the tales of Bishop Jacob and how he was able to perform miracles, he was furious. No, he would not allow another saint to interfere with his own work. He knew that the man they called Jacob would have to be dealt with swiftly. And though he knew that men such as this posed his greatest challenge, it was from just such a challenge that his greatest joy could be obtained.

The devil left the body of Barabbas and watched him collapse with satisfaction, for the man had been taken over completely. But still the devil needed him so he did not destroy him yet and only looked at him with apathy.

Yes the devil knew that Bishop Jacob was scouring the countryside looking for him, so he decided to allow himself to be found, or rather, he decided to bring him in closer. The Bishop would be looking for signs, so the devil decided to leave signs. Many of his past encounters with saints had ended badly for the devil, but not all. And many a saint had proven himself unworthy but for his encounter with the devil. In truth however, it was not the purpose of the devil to hate the men he possessed, and many of such men he had come to admire. The men were only his tools to be used for his true purpose, and that was to defy the Lord. It was the presence of the Lord that he could not abide, but oh, how he hated men who walked with the Lord.

The devil came to a new village and looked for a suitable body, for the body of

Barabbas was of little use to him now. For such work the devil travelled only in spirit, so he was able to go about unnoticed and observe the people very carefully. He watched people when they did not know they were being watched; he watched people in their private moments; he saw the people trying to hide their own faults, their failures, their misdeeds and their sin, and secretly he was proud of them. Now children were very difficult to possess because of their ignorance of sin, and elderly people were either too stubborn or not worth the effort to possess. Ideally, it was adults and young adults that served his purposes best, and they were easy to find. Men were easiest to target and to trick, but it was the women that were the most exquisite to possess. Every woman could be useful, but a beautiful, unmarried woman most especially.

It was late. The devil walked along a cart path leading into the village just as the sun was starting to set. A middle-aged woman was taking clothes down from a line strung across two trees, and the devil, being tired of walking, quickly decided that she would be good enough for a night . . . perhaps two. And when the devil entered her body she did not even notice because she was humming an old tune learned from her mother when she was a little girl.

Normally when the devil entered a body there would be resistance and he would have to fight hard to break their will, even as a young colt fights against the lash and the bridle. Sometimes the will to fight was so strong and so resolute that the person did not survive the attempt, and then the devil would have to search for a new host. A strong impulse to retch was the first manifestation of the devil's presence and the unsuspecting host usually became weaker from just such an impulse. This new woman had a strong will for he could feel it, but he had no intention of breaking her all at once, no, he only wanted to use her for a small part, a brief interlude, for his true intention was only to foment fear.

"Hurry, hurry!" cried Michael, the devout but flawed husband of his good wife Mariah. "It's getting dark, dear, hurry with your chores and come in for supper."

Mariah was walking slower this night because the devil was having some trouble getting her to move as he wanted. A few times she stumbled and the devil cursed, but the lips of Mariah only continued to hum her precious melody.

"Hurry dear," Michael cried again. "The soup is ready."

Mariah smiled and tried to walk faster and the devil let her have her way because he wasn't in the mood to fight with her just yet. So the devil bided his time and the devil went into the cottage for a supper of soup and bread. Then the devil lay dormant and listened to the mindless chatter of the man and his good wife. Yes, the devil was decidedly bored with such trite conversation, and after almost an hour of listening to the couple speaking of household chores and other quaint trivialities, he had had enough. He grabbed hold of the good woman's mind with an icy grip and violently forced her to speak.

"I wash your filthy clothes! I . . . I cook your miserable supper every day! I . . . I . . ., "but the poor woman broke down in tears and could not continue and even the devil could not hold her.

Michael could not believe the words that had come out of his wife's mouth. He saw her weeping, but he did not know that she was fighting such a malevolent adversary, for how could he have known? Instead, he heard her cries and her cries struck his heart like a hammer-blow and he became conscious of his own weakness. Yes, perhaps he expected too much from her, perhaps he had taken her good nature for granted and not as a gift, never realizing just how hard she worked. Instead of anger, Michael only took his good wife in his arms and held her, gently stroking her hair and speaking tender words.

Finally, the devil could take no more. Such signs of compassion only sickened him, and with great satisfaction he left the woman and, like a slap in the face, the devil's departure caused her visceral pain.

The next person the devil entered was a young boy lost in airy dreams. He offered no resistance, and the devil, wanting only to take a rest, allowed himself to rest until he should need the boy. So the devil hid away inside the boy and experienced the youthful vigor that came with innocence and ignorance and like a sleeping snake, went dormant.

Axel Stevenson was a good man, a godly man. He, along with his good wife and their son Axon, lived in peace by the word of God and the wool of their flock. Much of the land was heath and wild moorland, which was excellent for grazing sheep and other docile animals. Axel gave his sheep room to graze and to wander and to do all the wonderful things that sheep do when they are not being shorn or butchered. Unlike many of the great shepherds of the isle, Axel knew how to read and how to think about what he had just read, so he was more than suited for a quiet life devoted to shepherding sheep and studying the scriptures. And to his only son Axon he passed on his learning and his love of animals. And by the time that Axon was but a strapping lad he knew more about animal husbandry, thanks to his father, than anyone else on the north side of the island. Axel taught Axon how to read and together they studied the word of God and were themselves but an extension of that word. Axel was proud of his son, proud yet humbled, as but for the grace of God we are all devoured by evil even as a sheep is shorn.

And so Axon the boy grew up confident in his ability and proud of the man that gave those abilities to him. But like all children and though they work hard, there must be time for friends and there must be time for play. Axon's father knew this very well and he allowed Axon time away from chores to play with his friends and to make new friends. Now on top of the plateau there were other families and other farms and other flocks, so it was no surprise that Axon should meet another boy his own age. This boy was named Neal.

Neal loved his own father more than his own life, for it was his father that raised him and took care of him when his mother died when he was very young. So, coming to know about his mother only from the stories told to him by his father, Neal formed a strong bond with his father that could never be broken, and woe to any boy that should ever utter a foul word about his father.

The two boys came to learn of each other due to their shared interest in sheep's wool. And though their sheep grazed upon the same precipice under similar conditions, in truth there was much to learn about raising a good flock for the savvy buyer wanted only the finest wool. These secrets were closely held and carefully guarded by the father of each boy and each boy admired them very much.

One day as the boys sat together near the edge of the cliff overlooking the sea the talk turned to their sheep, for each boy thought of the flock as their own. It was a grey day and the fragrant wind coming from the sea was heady and brisk.

"I have the finest sheep on the island," said Neal. "And my sheep have the finest wool."

"Those are your father's sheep," Axon said to his boastful friend.

"They are my sheep," Neal corrected him. "My father knows everything, and he has taught me everything he knows."

Axon laughed.

"Do you think that is funny!" Neal snapped with anger.

"I think that you are funny," Axon replied. "And my father is greater than your father. That is why my sheep are better."

Then the two boys started to argue aggressively, and that is when the devil woke up inside Axon. Words turned to blows and soon the two boys were fighting wildly as they drew closer and closer to the precipice. Neal was by far the stronger boy and soon he had Axon backed up against the cliff. To fall would mean certain death. Neal took hold of Axon and shook him violently.

"My father is greater!" he cried. "Say it!"

Axon was frightened. He looked into the eyes of his fiery friend and saw the fierce pride, but he would not speak. Then Neal began to push him closer and closer to the edge as his anger grew. The devil saw into the boy's eyes and he was impressed, for this was an emotion that he understood very well. Now Neal held him even more tightly in his grip and with one hand struck him across the face.

"Say it!" he demanded.

Axon looked into the eyes of his adversary and they were cold and ruthless. Axon was totally unprepared for such an explosion of anger and he started to cry. When he started to cry the devil was so disappointed with him that he could no longer watch and he waited to see what would happen, for now he was hoping for the worst. But when Neal saw that Axon was not going to say what he wanted to hear he threw him down on the ground forcefully and walked away.

The dishonored boy lay for a long time with his eyes closed. He was hurt and he was ashamed for he had not defended himself and he had not defended his own father against the unjust accusations against him. Axon could not stop reflecting on his own shame, for how could he ever face his former friend again?

This is when the devil spoke to him. At first Axon thought the words were coming from his own mind and that the words were his own words, but slowly he came to know the truth.

"Just wait," the soft voice reassured him. "The time will come for you to show that you are justified. The time will come for you to hold your head up with pride, for you are wise, and you are terrible in your judgment. Don't worry, Axon, for I am with you."

"Are you the Lord?" Axon said with piety.

"Do not say my name," the devil replied. "Do not speak to me. When the time is right I will speak to you."

And so it was that Bishop Jacob next entered the small hamlet nestled on the cliffs overlooking the sea. He was drawn to the cliffs due to certain rumors he had heard. There were strange rumors of fallen and dismembered sheep, for the sheep of Ellin, father of Neal, were stricken with misfortune. The people were convinced that the devil was responsible for the slaughter, but they had no witnesses and they had no proof. Jacob was eager to hear the news for he had searched long and hard. The people sent him to talk with Axon because Axon watched over his own flock and he could easily see into the fields of Ellin, where his own son watched over the flock so carefully.

The devil watched the Bishop walking across the stony highland and he decided to study him carefully lest he make a critical mistake. He knew that the Bishop would have no reason to suspect his presence in the boy, but he had to remain alert. He relaxed his grip on the boy, but he remained cautious.

Now Axon watched Jacob with admiration of a kindred spirit, for his slow, methodical gate was the gate of a shepherd and his white cloak the raiment of a shepherd; and the long staff he carried was the staff of a shepherd and his windswept hair the hair of a shepherd. The Bishop was a man of God, a shepherd of God. In the boy's eyes, the Bishop was awesome in presence and an aura surrounded his actions like the faint radiance of afternoon light surrounding an icon.

The devil loosened his grip on the boy and the boy slowly recovered. His head ached and his memory returned like an echo from the past of which he had no recollection, and like a sleeper emerging from the heavy perfume of troubled slumber he came once again to know himself. Axon watched the Bishop thoughtfully but he could not remember how to speak, but when the Bishop was in earshot of the boy he spoke first and shattered the bonds of atrophy.

"A good day to you lad," the Bishop said. "Is your name Axon?"

"A good day to you as well," the boy replied. "My name is Axon, son of Axel."

"Your flock is magnificent."

"My father is a good shepherd," the boy replied with pride.

"And the field over yonder," said the Bishop, pointing to the field of Neal's father. "Fine animals they are. Yes, such fine sheep require a fine shepherd."

"Yes, that is true," Axon agreed.

"Do you know why anyone would want to harm such a fine flock?" Jacob said plainly. "I have heard stories told of terrible things done to his flock, but no one knows why anyone would want to do such harm because the shepherd is well liked."

"Tis a mystery," Axon answered.

"I pray that your flock has not been harmed," said Jacob.

"I continue to watch them carefully."

"And do not waver in your diligence, for I have heard strange talk of the devil. Some of the people are saying that he is responsible for the harm done to the sheep . . ., but I think that the devil is far too clever to attempt such an attack. No, that is not his way. It is far more likely that he has found someone else to do it for him."

Axon listened to the words of the Bishop and his eyes began to water. "I will do as you say," he replied. "I will be watchful."

Then Jacob turned and began walking back from whence he came. Suddenly Axon went lifeless as the devil erupted inside of him. The boy trembled uncontrollably before collapsing on the ground. The Bishop did not see this however, and he was almost across the plateau before they attacked. Then the sky turned dark and a roar of cackling noise blared from above as an enormous murder of crows filled the sky. Like a whirlwind they circled the Bishop, surrounding him, pecking and clawing and searching for flesh to rend.

Bishop Jacob fought valiantly, striking them violently and knocking them out of the sky. But the crows were driven by a force, a singular corruption that sought only to kill the Bishop. The Bishop was also driven by a singular force however, an inextricable force ignited by the power of the Lord. The crows continued attacking until the Bishop raised his arms to the sky and shouted a command and suddenly, like feathers falling from the mouth of a careless fox, the crows fell in singular destruction to the ground dead.

Then Bishop Jacob went back to check on the boy because now his suspicion had been confirmed. Axon was laying face down in a patch of yellow gorse. A few sheep were gathered around him as if they were worried. But what could they have known? Could they have guessed that the great deceiver was about, and would they have cared?

Axon was dazed. The devil no longer cared what happened to the boy for he was finished with him. The devil left him like a broken toy. Jacob bent down and touched the boy.

"Are you alright?" he asked.

The devil was gone; the boy's mind was free and clear. He looked into the eyes of the Bishop and he was ashamed.

"Forgive me," he cried. "I have sinned greatly."

"We are all sinners," Jacob replied. "The devil is gone from you now and you are safe. The devil has used you for ill, but you are free now."

"I want to follow you," Axon replied softly. "I will help you find and destroy . . . ."

"Your place is with your father and with your flock," Jacob responded. "Care for your flock as you care for those around you, as the word of Christ cares for us all."

The Bishop had hurt the devil, that is true, but mostly he had hurt his pride for once again his plans had been thwarted . . .interrupted. "I will bring this bishop down," said the devil with fury. "All men are mortal as all men are sinners. All men can be righteous for a moment. All men may do good when they may profit from goodness, but all men are weak."

And so the devil mused and mused upon the proper way to apply his plan. In truth, the devil had lost none of his cleverness when he had been cast down, and the blackness of his soul only became blacker but for his fall. And so the devil devised a plan, a plan so evil and contemptible that he could have smiled had he a face with which to smile.

The Torment of King Sigmus

King Sigmus felt a tightening in his stomach as he led the Bishop higher and higher, and the higher he climbed the greater his visceral dread became, for there were great forces at work and the King did not know the extent of his own guilt.

Now the devil knew that he would not be able to enter this man by force. No, he would need stealth, and he would need to use clever deception lest his plan fail completely. Most men were easy to enter, and though many men would be able to endure all but the most carnal temptations, they would prove to be disappointing and ultimately weak.

The King tossed and turned beneath the weight of a terrible dream, a nightmare. He was wandering through an inferno, a fiery hell, and his arms and legs would not obey his mind but instead seemed to follow the direction of someone else that was inside of him, controlling his body as a child controls a doll. The King woke with a sudden start and felt the need to pray.

Sigmus went to the window and felt a rush of cool air. He took a deep breath and felt strength returning to his body, but the strange aspect of his nightmare did not dissipate but only became stronger. Restless and fighting against the building sensation of doom, the King decided to take a walk. Many years had passed since last the King roamed the dark and empty halls of his castle in the wee hours of the night and he smiled when he remembered the comfort it used to bring him as he imagined Prince Bartholomew.

So into the dark corridors of his castle the King went on his way, thoughtless, carrying only a single candle for light. The corridors were long and empty mostly, sometimes guarded by empty suits of tarnished armor, but on the walls hung many tapestries and oil paintings from the low lands and pieces of historical weaponry. But it was not weapons and decaying gauntlets and artwork which most earnestly spoke to the King, no, indeed it was the portraits of past kings, including the portrait of his father, which meant most to him.

In a long corridor along an inner wall is where the portrait hung. Sigmus came here to be alone or to contemplate great issues, and his inspiration often came from the captured images of faded kings, faded campaigns, faded wisdom, faded memories, and faded love; this was a place where he could be judged by his equals, those that had rendered glory to their kingdom and those that had fallen into corruption, for it was in his nature for humility to guide his most profound decisions, for this is the way of the king and this is the way of the Lord.

The portrait of his father hung silently in the dim light, an apparition floating above and beyond the purely temporal, his great eyes staring gallantly out to sea. Sigmus looked long and hard at the painting and felt the comfort of the powerful memories that flooded into his mind like the tide from a supernatural realm beyond the sea. Sigmus relaxed as the many stories of his father flooded back to him now. He knew his father through the stories told to him by his tutors, and the stories became precious as the years ebbed and flowed and the memories became memories of memories. In truth, Sigmus had barely known his father. His father had died during a skirmish with a band of angry Scotsmen when he was but a child, and his father had been taken down after himself taking down five of the Scotsmen. It was said that he fought gallantly and without mercy. Yes, good King Thomas was a man of fiery action and not one to be taken without cost. In this way King Sigmus was elevated to the Crown without bloodshed, and never did he need to raise his sword in anger against an enemy, and he would never forget. The devil learned this as he probed the mind of the King. The same memories flooded into the mind of the devil. Sigmus continued to stare at the painting of his father, the penetrating eyes, the sharp jaw, the high, aristocratic cheek bone, and the image seemed to speak to him from beyond, and though the sound was inside of his head, Sigmus heard the voice of his father speaking to him.

"I love you father," Sigmus muttered softly into the dimness.

"Protect the realm," he heard distinctly in his head, but it was the voice of his father.

"The devil has come to lay waste," Sigmus replied thoughtfully. "Tell me what you want me to do, father. Tell me and I will do it."

"Protect the realm," the voice of his father repeated with even greater authority.

"From what?" Sigmus cried. "Tell me the danger that I may fight against it."

"Do not be deceived my son. There are those that would seek to perform miracles. Beware of miracles and miracle workers . . . be vigilant.

"The Lord works through miracles," Sigmus pleaded by way of justification of his own trepidation.

"The devil also works miracles" the voice of his father said sternly.

Sigmus suddenly fell to his knees. In the wavering light he looked up to the image of his father with tenderness and implored as a single tear fell from his eye.

"Speak to me father. Where are you? Are you in heaven? I am afraid. Can you tell me in words how to gain the strength to continue? I am weary and I want to be with you."

"Do not worry," said the devil through the tender memories of the King. "We shall be together when your time is finished, but you must not fail in the mission you have been left to perform on earth. Find the deceiver, my son. Root him out and protect the realm, but remember son and be wary, for the deceiver is clever."

The King went back to his bedchamber to sleep, but he was shaken to the core. His father had reached back from beyond and his message was clear. Sigmus had never heard voices until now and his apprehension was turning into fear, for if his father could reach out from beyond the grave then nothing in this world made any sense to him anymore. But his biggest fear was that he was being watched . . . judged.

At last Bishop Jacob arrived in Castletown. No children came out to meet him, no elders came out to greet him, and in truth his arrival would have gone completely unnoticed but for the presence of an old woman that stood near the edge of a cart path waiting for him. She was dressed in a long brown cloak that reached to the ground. Her head was hidden inside the shadow of her wide-brimmed hat. She smiled; several teeth were missing. The Bishop nodded respectfully.

"I have been watching for you," she said.

"I have wandered to and fro," said Jacob. "How came you to be waiting for me when I have been carried by the wind?"

"Your coming has been foretold," she answered. "I have seen you in a dream."

"Then you are wiser than I," answered Jacob.

"A wise man follows Christ."

"And a wise man flees from the devil," Jacob added. "Tell me my good woman, has the devil yet tainted Castletown with his presence?"

"You know that he has," she answered. "You would not be here were that not so, for you are drawn to his power, are you not?"

"Tell me then woman, where shall I find this loathsome creature?"

The old woman now became cryptic. "Turn over a stone and you shall find him," she said. "The devil enjoys suffering, so look for suffering and you shall find him."

Jacob looked closely at the woman and an alarm like the gentle tickling of a spider rose up within him. The woman was a seer and he had no time for seers, soothsayers and sorcerers.

"The devil likes blasphemy," the woman continued, "so look for those that blaspheme. And look at the men of pride, for the devil is proud."

Jacob was becoming irritated with the woman. "These things are in all places," he said. "But I am looking for the devil, not his minions and shepherds."

"He is here," the woman said with certainty. "He has been here for days now, walking, lurking in shadows, whispering, for I have felt his presence even as I felt your coming."

"Then tell me where he is and do not waylay my journey."

"You wear the clothing of a shepherd, and yet you are not a shepherd."

"No, I am not."

"The king has ordered that blasphemers be brought for trial, for such corruption can no longer be tolerated."

Jacob looked up suddenly. "King Sigmus gave this order?" he asked with disbelief.

"That is how the devil can be known . . . through the tongue. Evil can be known through the eyes, but it is through the hands and through the tongue that it is spread."

"Yet there are those that would say that all men are evil," said Jacob. "And there are those that would say that only by the grace of Christ can we be saved, for every moment of our life is sinful and abhorrent to the Lord."

"Are you a philosopher?"

"I am a servant," Jacob answered.

"The devil tempts us," the woman said by way of explanation. "But for the devil we would be righteous."

Bishop Jacob shook his head slowly as if he was pained by the woman's very words. "No," he said to her. "We are weak . . . all men are weak. Strength comes only through the grace of God. The devil is strong. The devil is very powerful. We must all of us, strengthen our soul through suffering, for only then will we know grace."

"Are you a saint?"

"I am a sinner."

"The devil loves suffering," the woman reiterated.

"And Christ loves those who would suffer," Jacob said. "Grace comes to us through suffering and to run from suffering is to run from the Lord."

Bishop Jacob walked along the narrow streets of Castletown like a man looking for something that is lost. If the devil lurked within he could not sense him, for the devil is a master of disguise. A man approached him asking for money even though he could see that the Bishop was far more destitute than he, a cart laden with vegetables passed by, a sullen woman contemplated an object behind a window, a stray dog sniffed at a curious puddle, a tired fisherman dragged a tangled net, somewhere in the distance a child cried, but Jacob could find no trace of the devil. Coming out of an inn, a man stumbled into the street and vomited.

And while Jacob looked around for traces of the devil, the people of Castletown looked around and saw Jacob, but they were not impressed by his manner of dress and his saintly appearance. On the contrary, they were suspicious of his movements and they watched to see what he would do. They watched from windows and from behind closed doors, they watched and they cocked an ear in case the strange man should speak.

Suddenly a rock struck Jacob in the back and he winced in pain. He turned to face his aggressor and another rock struck him in the head. The blow knocked him to his knees and he looked around warily to see from which quarter the attack was coming. The Bishop tasted blood in his mouth and his vision was becoming blurred, but he could see, walking directly at him a group of men, some old and some young, and they were wielding sticks. Then his world went black. When Jacob opened his eyes again he was in a strange bed.

An ordinary woman, common but for her striking beauty, jumped up from a chair in which she had been waiting for the Bishop to open his eyes. And when he did, the first thing he saw was her beautiful smile.

"Ah, Iona," he sighed through his dizziness. "Are you alright my dear?"

The question made her smile even more broadly. "Of course I am alright," she answered uneasily. "It is you that is hurt, not I."

Jacob started to get out of bed but fell back again for his head was heavy with weakness. It was then that he remembered the attack.

"What happened to me, Iona?"

"Some people are frightened of you," she answered, taking hold of his cold hand lightly.

"But I have hurt no one, Iona. Tell me, where is Sigmus? I must speak with him."

"He is meeting with those that have brought you here . . . they say that you are a sorcerer."

Jacob felt the warmth of Iona's hand and he felt comforted. "And what does Sigmus say?" he asked.

"Oh, Jacob I am frightened for you," she answered and Jacob could feel her delicate hand tremble. "Sigmus has changed. He talks about nothing but devils and sorcerers and he paces the empty corridors late at night when everyone is asleep. I am afraid for him, Jacob, as I am afraid for you. Sigmus says that you have changed . . . but."

Jacob listened but he was tired, so utterly tired, for he could not rest knowing that the devil was about. He felt great compassion for Iona, for he believed that she was a good woman and that her love of Christ was strong. Yes, he was aware of the unusual relationship between King Sigmus and Iona, his personal attendant, and he knew what the people must have thought. Yes, there were rumors, and yes, he was not so ignorant as to believe in outward appearances and to deny the need for physical as well as filial love. King Sigmus was not a saint, but he was righteous and his heart was pure. But Jacob could see that the poor woman was truly frightened and his heart warmed to her fear. He tried to comfort her.

"Fear not, Iona. The Lord has a plan for us all, and the Lord is not easily fooled by clever manipulations of the devil."

When Jacob opened his eyes again Sigmus was there. He must have fallen asleep again. He saw the face of his old friend, the square chin, the high forehead, the blonde hair now streaked with grey, and the deep, pale blue eyes looking down at him and his face was furrowed with the force of many questions.

"Are you feeling better now?" Sigmus asked. "You were beaten badly, Jacob. I want you to stay in bed for a few days to recover, for I think that you should rest. Your journey can continue when you are well again."

Jacob struggled to rise from his position and managed to elevate himself slightly against the headboard. He looked at his friend, the King, and he tried to smile, but something prevented such an expression. Instead, he felt uneasy but he did not know why.

"What has happened here, Sigmus? Talk to me."

"There will be time for talk," Sigmus said as a slight smile escaped him. "For now you must rest. I will leave you now my friend. You had me worried."

"Wait!" Jacob cried. "Before you go, Sigmus, tell me what has happened here."

King Sigmus gently took hold of Bishop Jacob and pushed him back down again and the Bishop offered no resistance. Then he went to the door, but before leaving he turned.

"Yes, Jacob, you were right. An old evil has invaded our home and, like a black smoke, brought death. These are times that try men's hearts, but we shall prevail."

King Sigmus closed the door behind him and then went to his bedchamber to put on his riding boots. He was feeling nauseous and his head ached. He closed his eyes and held his hands against his throbbing temples. Iona came into the room and watched him with sadness and waited for him to open his eyes.

"Ah, Iona," he said when he saw her. "What are you up to, young lady?"

Iona went down on her knees and helped him with his boots. She cautiously asked how he felt though she knew that he was in pain.

Sigmus took her hand and kissed it. "Thank you for asking, my dear. In truth, the pain subsides only to come back again with even more intensity."

"You need to be in bed, Sigmus. Please think about yourself for a minute and you will see that you cannot continue without rest."

"Does the devil rest?" Sigmus answered as he kissed her delicate hand again. "No Iona, a King does not rest when his kingdom is under siege."

"Tell me Sigmus, where are you off to now? The bishop is laying in bed and he needs us. You cannot abandon him now."

"I am only going away for the day," Sigmus replied, "perhaps two. You will watch over the bishop while I am gone. Tell him everything he wants to know, Iona. Only do not worry about me and do not give Jacob reason for worry either. I suspect that he has enough to worry about already."

Then the King took her hands and brought her to her feet. He kissed her without passion and there was a paleness in his expression. An unexpected pain surged through his head and he winced noticeably. Iona started to speak but Sigmus only pushed her away gently and then strode out of the room.

Iona followed quickly behind the King and caught up with him in the long corridor. She was worried for the King and she did not want him to go away from her, for she felt like she was losing him. She wrapped her arms around him and tried to hold him back.

"Oh, please Sigmus don't go away yet. Tell me a story. Please tell me a story so that I know that you are alright. I am frightened for you."

The King turned around and took his young mistress by the shoulders to comfort her and try to settle her fear. It was not like Iona to worry so the King weakened a bit.

"Alright," said Sigmus. "I will tell you the story about King Bartholomew . . ."

"No, no, no," Iona pleaded. "Not that, Sigmus. Do not begin again about . . ."

"Oh, Iona you silly girl, I am fine, but I will tell you a story so that you will not worry about me." Then the King looked into her beautiful eyes and with a familiar smile on his face he began.

Though Iona was struck dumb by her fear for the King, secretly she admired his bravery, his conquest of greater and more impossible feats, and she wished that she could descend the deep water to the abysmal depths and terrors that waited below. As expected, the lower and middle orders of the Manx were there to watch and cheer for the King after his successful dive in his newest contraption — a diving bell as it was being called.

This was during the fifth year of the reign of Bartholomew. Many curious Manxmen referred to him as Bartholomew the Restless, because of his tireless and singular propensity for exploration and adventure, but mostly for his utter folly and misadventure. There was great expectation for this new adventure by the King, now once again bored with the foxhunt and resuming his study into the field of ghosts and lost souls and satyrs, witches, wizards, lost sheep and infinity, after a period of indolence out of which he was only beginning to emerge. Food and beverages were brought down from Peel Castle in anticipation of a giant celebration that was to follow the King's success. Presently tables were being laden with breads, nuts, cheeses, roasted chicken, a slaughtered calf, grouse, beets, artichokes, potatoes, mulled wine, cinnamon, pies, pastries, fish soup, fish pie, fish custard, fish beverages, and noble fare to which the Manx were unaccustomed but for these adventures by the King. Tents were erected and children chased rabbits and lame dogs through the field, yes, this was truly a day for celebration.

This new folly of the King involved the penetration of the sea in an enclosed booth. Six of the strongest lads of Man were recruited to handle the block and tackle. They were given explicit instructions from the King, but from where he received his instructions none could say, openly. It was generally agreed that the sea floor was littered with a myriad of treasure that could make even a King blush, but the King declared that he was after something else and that rubies and topaz and Norse silver were of no use to him. The King's closest friends, even Bishop Jacob begged him to know what could be so important on the bottom of the sea to risk such an endeavor.

"Some people say that the sea is endless," said the King with a wink. "The sea is not endless," he replied. "Were the sea endless, there would be no place for the water to move and the sea would be frozen and unmovable. Everything comes to an end. All things come to an end, and that is precisely what I hope to discover."

Murmuring in the crowd spread. "The end of the world! The King is going to find the end of the world. Are you looking for the end of the world?" the excited voices of his subjects begged to know.

"All is one," replied the still smiling King, decked out in his most colorful tunic and purple gaiters for the occasion. "I am looking for the beginning of the world! The world is one thing," he said, "not two things or many. Everything is part of a single thing, a single event of spectacular consequence, and we are all reverberations."

"Hooray!" the people cheered, and even though they did not know what a reverberation was they cheered for the honor of being a reverberation. They all loved the King . . . even through his strange days.

Something of an amateur inventor, the King designed all his own contraptions. Most failed, but the failure was usually in such spectacular fashion that the King endeared himself to the simple people of Man, for failure to the simple man is a sign that God is watching. His Sea Urchin, as he always referred to it, was encased in metal because of the intense cold and pressure and the possibility of attack beneath the waves that his endeavor presupposed. The Urchin had a single small window from which the King would see the watery depths of his kingdom. Inside the Urchin was very different from what was hinted at by the tortoise shell of a hull that enclosed it. One thing that was absolutely necessary for the King to be able to make all the many decisions beneath the waves was a comfortable chair, so the Urchin was supplied with a comfortable chair. Most of the other equipment was mysterious and secret. The King also designed these instruments, as they were called, although he had some help from an unknown source that lived in the interior of the island and was reputed to be a wizard. Other folk believed that he was an ancient alchemist or hermetic philosopher because of the strange light that sometimes could be seen emanating from his solitary window that looked out to the sea. Perhaps he consulted with antediluvian creatures that lived in the sea, none could say, but every few years another story would emerge and be debated into the wee hours of the night in the taverns of Man. The blacksmith shook his head and refused to speak about the strange smoke that could be seen coming from his shed. All that he would ever say was, "That was a curious smoke for an honest man. The color was all wrong, but the smell was very curious." But as for the instruments, no one knew what purpose so many levers and dials and glass-enclosed instruments and gears could have at the bottom of the sea, and the King kept this secret safe.

With a salvo of cheers and oaths and the breaking of glass and the scattering of seeds and wheat and corner-dust, the King disappeared beneath the waves with a smile and vanished into the murkiness. The strong lads lowered the King slowly and carefully. A single tug from a line controlled by the King would indicate that they were to lower him faster. A double tug would mean to slow down his descent. Three quick tugs would mean to stop, and four quick tugs would mean to abandon all prudence and raise him back to the surface.

The first few leagues were uneventful and but for the sight of a shark or an eel or a giant flounder the King would have died from boredom. Down he went into the unknown depths from which no man had ever returned. After a few hundred leagues, however, the scenery began to change, and as if he had suddenly entered a new season or unknown constellation, the temperature plunged and the King had to put on a woolen sweater. At these depths the sea creatures changed as if a different zone had now been reached. A giant sea horse nearly collided with the Urchin causing the King to spill his tea and he tugged on the rope to slow his descent. It was time to pay closer attention.

Now the sea began to brighten with an uncanny iridescence from beyond the scope of his limited vision. Sea plants and schools of glowing shrimp drifted past his window and for a moment the King thought he saw millions of tiny translucent eyes watching him. Down he went, emerging for a moment into a ring of underwater life only to suddenly once again be plunged into nothingness. The sea was filled with layers and layers of separate systems of complicated life patterns that was not unlike the mysterious rings of Saturn so speculated about by the astrologers and necromancers.

Suddenly something attached itself to the Urchin with a small impact and a thud. The King put his face against the cold glass to get a better look but the surrounding sea was teeming with infinitesimally small life and his vision was fuzzy. He peered through the cloudy glass and had to wipe the condensation away continuously. Then with a jolt he saw a hideous face staring at him from outside the Urchin. It was a monster! So frightened was the King that he tugged at the rope several times before he realized that he couldn't remember the code he had instructed to the lads up top. The Urchin plunged violently as if he had accidentally given the signal to cut the line. Down he went. Something was terribly wrong. Down down down, faster and faster the Urchin plunged. The King pulled the rope with all his strength and it snapped. Side to side the King was pitched as the Urchin sunk to its perdition. There was nothing to be done.

Then the Urchin crashed into the sea floor and stopped violently and the King was pitched to the floor. He lay still and waited for the side of the Urchin to implode, but it remained solid. The King was alive, but the King was in mortal danger. Now he was burning with an inner heat and the window was completely fogged up. Never before had he known such suffocating silence, and he knew that the silence of the grave could not differ noticeably from this watery isolation and that the two were one.

The King went to the window and wiped away the fog. No more than thirty meters from his position he could see a trail of giant lobsters coming directly for the Urchin. They were treading along in perfect formation, the way an army or an honor guard would march. Suddenly they broke formation and formed two groups that quickly flanked the Urchin fore and aft. Then the largest lobster, the King quickly surmised that this would be the leader, went to the window and with its giant pincer pounded on the hull of the Urchin. Startled, the King recoiled, but when the lobster continued to hammer on the hull, the King knew that the vessel would be torn apart if he did not acknowledge. Fearing that he may lose his only chance to survive, the King sat down in his chair and grabbed hold of a set of levers that were designed for just such a predicament. And so began the great lobster battle with the King of the Manx. The King cranked a wheel extending a pair of long, mandible like pincers toward an already excited creature. They immediately locked claws and a great battle ensued. The lobster fought hard, but his crushing, tearing, pinching vices could not damage the metal arms of the Urchin. The lobster freed itself from the grasp of the King and disappeared around the corner out of sight. Suddenly the King felt his vessel being lifted off the floor and he realized that he was being transported on the back of a company of lobsters. There was nothing he could do except wait.

They took him a short distance across the agitated seabed and entered a crevice that was concealed between a rock formation. Slowly the water began to clear and the King could see where he was being taken. Up a short platform they went. The urchin was set down and a long procession of lobsters could be seen retreating. Then, before the King could even move or scratch his beard, the hatch was opened and the face of a man peered down into the compartment.

"Hello there," said the man. "Please come out here, it is really quite safe and I think you will find the air quality much to your satisfaction."

The King was astonished. "Where is the water?" he shouted.

"There is no water in this Kingdom," said the man. "Unless you would like to see our lake which we use for bathing."

"Who are you?" demanded the King. "I am the King of the Manx, and I demand to know to whom I am speaking."

"You are far from home," said the man. "You do not belong here, so it is you who are trespassing, and I should demand an explanation from you. My name is Archeon if you must know."

The King softened. "Forgive my choice of words," he said. "I am on an adventure, and as you can see . . . well, it has not turned out for the best."

"That is true." said Archeon.

"Is this the end of the world?" said the King. "Have I reached the end of the world?"

The man laughed. "No sir, you have absolutely not reached the end of the world. That is on the other side of my Kingdom, and if you would like me to take you there . . . but I do not think you really want to go there. You are still living, I pray?"

"Yes. Yes, indeed, I am still living," said the King. "Why do you not wish to take me there?"

Archeon smiled sheepishly. "You do not belong here. This is a most extraordinary breach of ethics, but I will tell you a secret, and then you must go home. You have come to the land of lost souls. This is the land where all lost souls go before they are taken to their destination."

"What do they do here?" asked the King.

"They wait," said Archeon. "They wait and they dream about what they will do back on earth if they ever get there."

"On earth?" said the King with trepidation.

"Come with me," said Archeon.

And then he began to walk out toward the sea where the lobsters went. The King followed. Archeon walked very slowly and stately. He led the King along a thick carpet into a dim room. Then he turned.

"It is almost time for you to leave," said Archeon. "Do not attempt to come back again. Do you understand?"

"Just tell me one thing," said the King with as much humility as he could muster.

"Ask, if you must," said Archeon, with growing impatience.

"Is this the land of the dead? Is this where I will go when I am no longer living?"

Archeon thought for a moment. Then he answered. "Know this," he said. "You have entered the land of the living, not the land of the dead. You have been given a chance to go back home again from a place which no other man has ever left alive."

"I don't understand," said the King. "What is this place, for heaven's sake tell me where I am."

Archeon was very apprehensive. "I fear only that I will tell you too much and that in some way I may do you more harm than good. This is a difficult subject to introduce, you must understand."

"These lost souls, Archeon . . . tell me, are they dead?"

"They have lost their body," said Archeon.

"Where is their body?" begged the King. "I must know."

"Their body is in your world," said Archeon. "This is the place where souls go when they can no longer recognize their own body and their own life. They wander here, sometimes forever, or until their body calls them back when they are . . ."

"Dead?" cried the King in horror.

Then Archeon put his hand in his pocket and brought it out. In it was a coin. He stretched out the coin to the King and held it there for him to take.

"Keep this coin in your pocket," he said. "It is magic. The next time you meet me you must show me this coin so that I will remember you. If you ever begin to forget your body, you must rub this coin for it will save you. I hope that I will never see you again. Farewell, King of the Manx."

Archeon turned quickly and walked down the carpet from which he and the King had come. Then he raised his hand and waved, and when he did this, suddenly the walls collapsed and the King was thrust into total darkness. Then he felt the floor beneath his feet move and he fell in the sudden, shifting, confusion. The carpet was wet! When the King felt it he thought that it felt like flesh of a peculiar kind. Then everything turned to chaos and motion and more confusion. He had the feeling that he was moving at great speed. This lasted only a few minutes until it stopped. Then the walls slowly opened, and the King now knew where he was. What he took to be a wall was the giant maw of a whale and the red carpet, a tongue. He started to protest when his breath was knocked out of his body by a great concussion and he was hurtled through the air and went crashing down on the Isle of Man, and so ended the adventure of King Bartholomew and the island of lost souls.

When King Sigmus finished his story he brought his hand to his head as the persistent pain in his head returned again. Iona watched the King and her fear turned to sympathy. Then the King smiled again and kissed her before turning and walking away. And this time Iona did not follow.

South of Kirk Maughold, on a high plateau overlooking the sea, is a small stone cottage built from the ancient crumbling ruins of a hill fort dating to before the coming of the Celtic people from across the Irish Sea, a time when invading forces fought bitterly, a time long before the saints. The wind and rain batter the cottage mercilessly while the solitary hermit inside shivers on cold nights and prays an endless succession of prayers.

Inside the lonely cottage, which be little more than a hut, lives the hermit Clement, Clement the Hermit he is called. The people leave him in peace to pray and they do not harass him and they do not burden him with their own needs. It is enough for them to see the little curling wisps of smoke that float from his stone chimney and take comfort, for they know that he is deep in prayer and they know that through prayer the intercession of the Lord can sometimes come. And so it is that Clement prays, but he does not pray for himself, indeed, his prayers are for the people all around that are too tired, too lazy, too selfish, and too ignorant to pray for themselves. Yes, in this Clement spends his time, and in this Clement offers himself, notwithstanding his own weakness.

Sigmus met him several years ago while traveling on one of his excursions. He wondered that such a feeble hut should be built so high upon the precipice without protection, and his curiosity was peaked. Thinking that the hut was an abandoned ruin, he left his horse and walked up to explore the site. He peered into the open window and was shocked to find that it was indeed occupied by a strange man that was kneeling in the middle of the room. Sigmus started to back away quietly.

"Wait!" the stern voice of the man exclaimed loudly.

Sigmus stopped. And like a man caught in the act of a misdeed, he waited for the man to speak.

"You are the King. I am at your service."

"I did not mean to disturb you while you were praying," Sigmus answered. "Perhaps I can return when you are not occupied."

"I am always occupied," said the man. "My life is prayer."

The King was confused. "Do you pray to be forgiven? For how many sins can one man commit for which to live a life of perpetual prayer?"

"Every thought and every word not spoken in the name of Christ is a sin."

"It is a very difficult life you have endeavored to live," said the King. "I wish you happiness and success in your work, and I remain forever at your service."

Then the King turned his back on the bewildered man and began to walk away. In a moment he heard the final words from the man.

"I will pray for you Sigmus, that you be strong and that you be blessed in your own work . . . until we meet again."

And now the King approached the small cottage again after so many years, but his memory remained true. And once again looking through the open window he saw the hermit in prayer. Sigmus watched without speaking for it was not his intention to disturb the devotions of any man so diligent in such work. In a moment Clement the Hermit opened his eyes and looked up as the presence of the King became known to him.

"So we meet again," he said with a smile. "Come around to the door. I have nothing to offer you, I am afraid, but I can offer you company if that is your desire."

"And I am still at your service," the King responded as the memory came back fully to him. "It is I that has something to offer you," he said with a smile. "That is, unless you have completely given up food and drink."

"No my friend, I am not so strong as you suppose and I eat more often than I would like."

Soon they were sitting together sharing a frugal but tasty makeshift lunch from the King's saddlebags. Clement was old and his years of asceticism had made him gaunt, but he was far from feeble and Sigmus was impressed with his vitality. The ascetic ate little, consuming hardly more than a tiny bird, and he drank only a sip of the strong ale. Sigmus was not offended in the least, for if truth be told he was apprehensive about offering anything at all because he knew of the strange predilections of solitary men who sometimes preferred dead weeds and locusts to soft bread.

After the meal was finished the King spoke. In truth he had come not for a visit, but for another reason. They went to the window and the King lit his pipe. Then he looked up and spoke.

"You are the closest thing to a saint that I know of," the King began.

Clement frowned. The King saw it and quickly tried to retract his statement for he had not thought to offend the hermit.

"Tell me Clement. Tell me in truth, what is a saint?"

The frown turned to a smile as Clement pondered the strange words of the King. The smile was so unassuming and sublime that the King relaxed.

"Strictly speaking, every man that heeds the words of the Lord is a saint and if he could thus refrain from speaking and from thinking he should thus remain a saint. But when one is forced to live in the world one quickly turns deaf to the words of the Lord."

"And that is why you live in isolation?" Sigmus asked.

"To live like a coward does not glorify the Lord, my friend. I do not hide from the world that my soul should remain strong."

"But you do not live in the world," Sigmus interrupted.

"My will is not my own," Clement said casually. "The Lord has not chosen to send me away from here, and so I stay."

"Your words are troubling to me," Sigmus said candidly. "Can we truly know the plan of the Lord? And if we should . . . then it is better never to act, but to remain docile as a lamb, for to act is to deafen our own ears."

"Now your words too are troubling, my friend. What you see before you is not all there is, but all that we are allowed to see though our instruments would seek to probe further. The world of God is not the world of men, Sigmus. The world of men is but a skin, covering up with indifferent completeness, the subtle world of God beneath the surface."

"And beneath the surface," Sigmus postulated, "is where the saints work their miracles? And yet, we can never see beneath this surface, so tell me then . . . how do the saints draw from this infinite world of miracles?"

"Are miracles so important to you, Sigmus? There are miracles all around you and yet you watch and ponder the imponderable, and still you fail to see that the entire world is a miracle."

The King's temper only became darker and more cynical as he listened to the words of Clement, for the presence of the devil, like a growing malignancy, was making him sick. He spat the words.

"It is very difficult to distinguish true miracle if everything is miraculous. Is the birth of a child such a miracle? And yet, the animals take no notice. Is every sunrise just such a miracle? Is every drop of rain, every sound, every morsel of food . . .?"

The King stopped abruptly. Clement watched him closely but remained silent. He knew that the King had more to say. Finally the King spoke again, but the bile was absent from his words.

"Show me this world of God, Clement. Show me this submerged domain of God. Tell me, how do I enter this place?"

"One does not enter this place," Clement answered. "This place enters you, for even as a rain barrel is filled during a storm, so shall you be filled with the power of Christ."

The devil snapped to attention at the mention of the hated word. He was so tired of such talk, of such devotion, of such righteousness, and he felt only bitterness, but not the sweet bitterness that he wrought through his own vileness. The devil tried to imagine to what end the King questioned this worthless man, but as yet he had no idea.

"And one becomes filled with the power to perform miracles?" Sigmus asked even as the devil tried to control him.

"The power of God is everywhere. Yes, it is submerged, but it is submerged within the heart of all men and all women, for such is the power of God that nothing, no eternal time or place can contain it . . .not a single man, nor the collective soul of every man born into eternity."

The devil took hold of Sigmus and forced him to speak. "Does it reach into the abyss?" he asked.

Clement was surprised by the question. He looked thoughtfully into the eyes of the King, causing the devil to retreat. "That is a strange question," he said. "Is something troubling you?"

The devil stayed back and Sigmus spoke for himself. "I did not mean to say that," he said. "I care nothing for the abyss."

"Remember," Clement said. "The saints do not work through the Lord. Rather, it is the Lord that chooses to work through the saints. And remember, the power of the Lord is limitless. But beware, for the devil can imitate many acts of the Lord. Do not be fooled by such deception, for such deception brings only death and misery."

"Then the saint does not act out of his own free will, but is compelled against his own will to act?"

"No Sigmus, that is not so. All men have a choice to follow the commandments of the Lord. And though they may be great or small, to the Lord all is one."

The King's reply was derisive. "And your choice is to pray," he said scornfully. "Other men toil endlessly and tirelessly work the sea for food, but for you it is enough only to pray?"

"The smallest creature is never lost to the Lord. Yes, the Lord may judge me too weak, too fragile, too unworthy, that is true. The weakest cry does not go unnoticed though our ears remain deaf to the sound of the Lord. Even the unshed tears of a baby are not lost to the Lord. It is only our own ears that tremble."

And now the devil was furious when he forced Sigmus to say, "Does the Lord prefer sheep to men?"

But Clement was not offended and only replied. "If I could be as the tiniest, the weakest, the smallest sparrow, I should consider myself honored to sing but a song for the Lord. If only we could all of us be content to sing our feeble praises to the Lord, how sweet that would be and we could want for nothing more."

The devil revolted inside the body of the King. "Are you saying that to God we are but songbirds? Songbirds!" he shouted with growing anger.

"Is your pride so great that you should refuse to sing to the Lord?"

The devil was nearly jumping out of the skin of the King for so great was his ire. The King began to lose control of his own thoughts as the devil asserted control and the words of the King became the words of the devil.

"I am no songbird!" he said forcefully.

Clement noted the change in the King, but he did not guess the truth. Instead, he only said. "Yes, I am of no consequence that is true, so I am content to sing the praises of the Lord with the meek voice I have been given. But other men have been given a gift, this also is true. These men are inspired by the Lord, and they are able to sing thus in their own voice. Yes, that can be beautiful as well. Are you one of these men, Sigmus?"

The devil, inside the body of the King, lashed out and struck the hermit in the face, knocking him to the floor. He raised his foot and would have smashed the fallen hermit but the King's will proved stronger. Sigmus went down on one knee and helped the dazed man to his feet. The King was shaking in the wake of his uncontrollable violence to the hermit.

"Forgive me!" he cried, trembling slightly. "Forgive me, Clement. I have brought dishonor to your door." The King was revolted by his own action and vowed to ask forgiveness, but his headache was becoming unbearable.

The devil quickly loosened his grip on the mind of the King lest he damage him. Yes, he had lost his temper and he had lost control, but only for a moment. The King was strong, and he was not under complete control yet. He had to be careful now lest he destroy the mind of the King and he be of no further use. If not for that blasted holy man the King would already be subjugated completely, he would make a note to deal with him later in due time, but for now his concern was for the Bishop.

The Bishop's Conversation with the Devil

Even as the body can become numb, so too can the mind, but unlike the numbness of the body, the mind only isolates us further until we become insensate and comfortable with our own weakness.

Jacob fell in and out of troubled sleep, and when he opened his eyes King Sigmus was seated at his bedside and his eyes were weary and glassy, for it was the devil that looked through them and carefully considered the convalescing bishop. The devil however did not want to kill the Bishop, for he held no malice toward him. His desire was only to use the Bishop for his own purpose; one of punishing the one for whom the Bishop lived and breathed, and of whose name he was powerless to utter. The devil was safe however, for the King was pushed back, asleep and insensate within his own mind for he could be controlled more easily at night. A candle burned faintly, but it was enough for the devil to study the bishop, and when Jacob opened his eyes the devil smiled through the face of the King, but the devil was careful not to rouse the sleeping sovereign and Jacob was too weak to comprehend, for even as the witch of Endor had channeled the words of Samuel, so too had the words of the dormant King channeled his own words for his diabolical purpose.

"How long have you been here?" Jacob asked softly through the torpor of interrupted sleep.

"I have been beside you all night," the devil replied.

"You must rest, Sigmus. I am fine."

"No, you have been badly injured," said the devil. "I will find those responsible for this outrage and have them quartered."

Jacob tried to rise in his bed for he was shocked. "No, no, Sigmus, this is not necessary. I beg you please do not do this for my sake, for I will recover."

"And my kingdom?" the devil replied. "Will my kingdom recover if I stand and do nothing?"

"These are strange times, Sigmus. Something evil has been unleashed upon our fair island. The people are frightened."

"Some people are saying that the devil is here, Jacob. What do you say?"

"Yes, yes" Jacob replied, "this is the work of the *deceiver*. But I will find him and I will cast him out, Sigmus. The devil is powerful, but the Lord is infinitely more powerful. The devil will make a mistake, and I will be there to catch him when he does."

The devil could not resist baiting the bishop so great was his pride in his own ability. "The devil is clever, Jacob. Beware that his powers be underestimated. The devil is ruthless, and it is his wont to attack those most innocent and helpless. This is how his presence is known, and this is how his terror is spread."

"How do you know so much about this creature, Sigmus?"

"I have seen what he can do," the devil replied. "He is most likely to slaughter the lamb in the midst of the entire flock, for this is his method. Are you not a shepherd, Jacob?"

Bishop Jacob seemed to consider carefully, for he did not answer right away. At last he spoke.

"Yes, Sigmus, perhaps I am a shepherd as well, but I have abandoned my flock in order to protect them . . . and now I wonder if I have erred."

The devil became alert. "How so, Jacob?" he said skillfully. "You have walked many miles in your quest. You can not be in all places at once."

"I was thinking about little Maria," Jacob replied. "I fear for her . . . and yet I walked away from her in her greatest need. I must go to her, Sigmus."

"Maria is not your concern, Jacob. She is but one little girl, but the malignancy is spreading throughout the entire island. It is better that you continue your quest and leave her fate to . . ."

"No, no Sigmus, I will not do that. As you say, what shepherd would leave his most vulnerable sheep to the mercy of wolves?"

"You are in no position to protect your flock when you are being attacked by your very own people, Jacob. Perhaps the people have made their choice and their choice is to go back to the old ways."

Jacob was very uncomfortable with the words of the King, and he said so. "You of all people, Sigmus, I would never have questioned . . . but what you are saying now I cannot sanction."

"Would that be so bad, Jacob, if the people fell into damnation? If the people damn themselves, you are not damned with them and you shall not suffer for what you have not done."

"You are unwell," Jacob said sadly. "You are not yourself, Sigmus, for the man I knew would never say, much less think, such baleful words. But, your words have made me tired, my friend, and I must sleep, for tomorrow I leave for Bishopscourt."

The Bishop's eyes began to flutter as sleep slowly overcame him, but the last words of the King would stick in his mind and give him no comfort. The King started to talk and his words wove a powerful spell within the mind of the Bishop.

"The evil you seek is transitory," the devil began. "The evil that you seek does not exist and therefore you will never find it. Evil cannot, and does not exist, for were it to exist it must needs have been created, and a good God cannot create something that is evil unless that God too be evil, but if such evil be not created it must needs exist before creation. Evil is outside of time and outside of place, and that is why you will never find it . . ."

Bishop Jacob opened his eyes with a powerful sense of urgency. The room was light though the candle had long burned out. He could still smell the acrid smoke. The King still sat beside him but he too was asleep. The last words of the King still resonated in his mind, unless perhaps he had dreamed them. Suddenly the King opened his eyes.

"Good morning, Jacob" Sigmus said, and though he was very tired he managed a smile. "I will have food brought for you, for you must be very hungry."

"Thank you Sigmus," Jacob replied, "but I will try to get up for I must be on my way soon."

Sigmus started to scowl but quickly smiled to disguise it. "Where are you off to?" he asked. "You need to recover my friend, at least for another day or two."

"I told you that I am worried about Maria," Jacob replied. "I must go to her, Sigmus, for I fear she is in danger."

This time the King did scowl. "Who is Maria?" he asked.

"Surely you remember, Sigmus. We talked about it last night."

"I am going with you," Sigmus said with resignation. "I cannot allow you to travel alone when you are hurt."

Then Sigmus stood up and went to the door. Turning back to the Bishop, he said:

"But we will eat first, Jacob. I insist."

A few minutes later the King was back at the door just as Bishop Jacob was coming out. His raiment had been cleaned but now the Bishop looked strangely odd so attired. The King took him gently by the arm and led him to a nearby table where breakfast was being arranged.

The path to Bishopscourt was rocky but well worn and they walked the horses at a leisurely pace because Sigmus would not allow the horses to go faster lest the Bishop fall and reinjure himself. Lost in thought, Jacob sat on his horse and allowed his mount to follow the King and he silently prayed to clear his mind. The King was content to walk along without speaking, for he was lost in his own thoughts, thoughts of ambivalence and thoughts of disconnection. He knew that something was terribly wrong with him, but he did not want to discuss the particulars of his own weakness with the Bishop, for a king is supposed to bring comfort to those around him and not be subjugated by small infirmities.

Late in the afternoon they stopped at an inn to eat lunch and to rest the horses. The sign hanging outside said *The Blue Kipper*. Through a wooden gate, they passed on to the two storey inn with high, peaked roofs and thick leaded glass windows. Jacob followed without question and he did not question the decision to stop even though they could have reached Bishopscourt long before dusk. Just outside of Peel Harbor is a small village devoted to curing and processing the famous Manx kippers. The King in his younger days came often to rest and to enjoy the wonderful kippers. Well known throughout the kingdom, the people knew the King well and stopped what they were doing to watch him dismount and to see what he would do next. They looked at the Bishop and they scratched their heads together, for not a one of them knew what to think of such a strange looking man and they did not know he was the Bishop.

"See that the horses get watered," said King Sigmus to a young boy that came running out in case an order be given.

A plate piled high with fried kippers and eggs was brought. The King ordered ale, but the Bishop asked for tea. Seated alone in an alcove away from the main dining area the two men set about eating.

"Now tell me," said Sigmus after filling his mouth with food. "What do you think is happening in my kingdom? Do not spare my feelings, for I know much already and it may be that I shall have to spare your feelings."

The Bishop ate much more slowly than the King, for his appetite and his tolerance for food was slowly fading. He nibbled on a small piece of fish and replied:

"Hardly so, my friend, for my feelings are raw, this is true. Yes, I too have seen death and it grieves me greatly."

"Is this the work of a necromancer?" Sigmus interrupted eagerly. "I know that strange men inhabit this island."

"No, Sigmus, this is not the work of a necromancer . . . oh that it were. What we face is even more foul than the greatest necromancer. Our fight is with the devil."

Suddenly the King started to choke violently. He drained his glass with a single gulp and waited for the spasm to subside.

"Yes, Sigmus, it is true," Jacob continued.

The King shook his head and rubbed his temples. "I am sorry," he said, "for I suddenly felt faint, but I am better now. Tell me more, Jacob."

"This is a dangerous foe, Sigmus. The devil is vile and the devil is powerful. This creature hates all men, but most especially righteous men. My fear is that this unholy menace has been summoned here for a reason."

"Is he in search of a righteous man, Jacob?" Sigmus asked.

"In the eyes of God a righteous man is rare, Sigmus. But in the eyes of the devil a righteous man is like a jewel set in a crown of jewels, and the devil wears his crown with pride. The devil seeks to disgrace the *creation* of the Lord, and it may be that the devil would seek to spoil the feast to bring misery to the host. The devil is clever, however, and it may be that we will not guess his purpose until it is too late."

"What kind of man summons the devil, Jacob?" asked Sigmus, but in his heart he already knew of one such man.

Men can become corrupt in their quest for money and power. The devil is wont to search out these men, and when he finds one he will offer a bargain. But the devil is a liar, Sigmus. The great deceiver always hides his true purpose and woe to the man caught in his snare."

Then a lumbering and awkward man approached the table at which Sigmus and Jacob sat talking and he carried with him a plate. The plate was empty. The King looked at the man with a question but the man was looking at the Bishop. With recognition in his eyes, the man looked at the Bishop though the Bishop had never seen him before. Suddenly the man spat onto the plate and set it before the Bishop, and when Jacob looked up into his face the man spat in his face.

With unimaginable speed, the King pushed himself away from the table and grabbed the man violently, striking him in the face with such a powerful blow that the man fell to the floor senseless. Then Sigmus took the plate in his hands and smashed it on the floor. Just then the proprietor stormed into the room to see what had happened.

"Who is this man?" Sigmus demanded, pointing down to the unconscious man beneath them.

But even as the King was speaking, the man woke up and tried to rise to his feet. He was dazed and disoriented.

"What happened to me?" the man asked with a look of confusion.

The King pointed to the Bishop. "Do you know who this is?" he demanded.

Clearly the man did not know. "Who are you?" he replied. "I was walking . . . and then I was here."

Bishop Jacob had wiped his face clean and he now looked carefully at the frightened man. "You are safe now," he said. "No further harm will come to you. Rise now and go about your business."

King Sigmus started to protest but the Bishop stopped him. "It was not his fault," the Bishop said with conviction. "We must leave here at once for we are being watched" And he looked at the King in a way that could leave no uncertainty about what he meant.

The two men rode away from the inn without speaking the words that were in their mind. After they were in open country and away from those who could overhear them they spoke candidly and without fear.

"Why did you stop me?" asked Sigmus. "I would have had him punished."

"Yes, Sigmus, that is true, but in truth it was not he that committed the act, and you would have punished an innocent man. He was but an instrument, I fear, and to have punished him would have given the devil much pleasure."

"Are you saying that the devil caused that man to do what he did to you?"

"You saw his eyes, Sigmus. That man did not even know what happened to him. He was an instrument of the devil even as a song is made recognizable based upon which instrument is used. Not all songs can needs be sung through the throats of sparrows, Sigmus, nor does the sparrow refuse to sing."

Later that day they rode out together across the great plateau above Peel Harbor and the crashing Western Sea below. They went along the coastal path toward Kirk Michael and Bishop Jacob looked to see the children at play and he wondered that they did not come out to meet him as they usually did. Bishop Jacob prayed silently for strength and to the saints and that they guide his actions. The gentle swaying of the horse comforted him.

And then they came out to meet him, at first one and then many. They gathered around him and the Bishop had to stop his horse. The children looked up to the Bishop and there was fear in their eyes.

"Poor Maria has died," they cried. "You must go to her and make her well."

"What are you saying?" the Bishop cried. "How long ago did she die?"

"She died yesterday," they said together. "Please go to her before it is too late," they cried, and the tears streamed down their faces.

The Bishop trotted away across the precipice furiously, with the King
following close behind. In front of a small cottage, the Bishop brought his
horse to a halt and tied the reins to a fence post. The cottage was dark inside as
all the shades were pulled down except for one small window near the back of
the house where little Maria slept; and that window was open and bright
colored curtains rustled in the wind. Jacob stood before the house and tried to
calm his nerves lest he further frighten the already grief-stricken mother.

The door opened slowly and a plump and hunched woman emerged. She
looked at the Bishop with recognition in her eyes, but they were exhausted and
teary. She knew the Bishop and she knew how much he loved the children.
The woman wrung her hands together but she could not speak through her
grief. The Bishop looked up to heaven and then back down to the poor
woman. Then the woman stepped aside to allow the Bishop to enter the
cottage but she did not meet his eyes. The Bishop walked past her without a
word and went straight to the small room in the back of the house. He opened
the door and went inside.

And there lay Maria on the bed almost as if she were sleeping. She was
dressed in a white dress, her Sunday best, and her hands were folded against
her body. The room smelled of death. Jacob looked down at her body and was
overcome with sadness. She was so young, so beautiful, and in her death
pallor she looked like an innocent child. The tears began to stream down the
face of the Bishop but he was not embarrassed and he did not wipe them away.
He gave no thought to how she could have died for his mind was numb to the
horror before him. He looked up to heaven once more and closed his eyes.
And now a silent fury rose up within his mind and he did not try to control it.
Slowly he walked to the bedside just as the King entered the room and what
the King saw next he would never forget.

The Bishop raised his arms to heaven and spoke. "Rise Maria," he said.
"Wake and rise Maria for you are not dead!"

And to the astonishment of the King, the dead child did open her dead eyes for
the Bishop had called her back from death. The Bishop did not see her for he
was still looking up to heaven, but suddenly he heard her soft voice speak and
he nearly collapsed. The King gasped and staggered backward from the shock
he had been given. And when the mother stormed into the room, she too was
frightened unto death, for before her stood her little girl, Maria.

News of the miracle traveled faster than the Bishop as he rode away slowly
from the cottage amidst tears of joy and praises to the Almighty. The King

rode beside him but he still could not speak, so the two men rode away in silence.

𝕿𝖍𝖊 𝕯𝖊𝖈𝖊𝖎𝖛𝖊𝖗

At last they reached the iron door behind which the final prisoner waited death. The Bishop waited for the King to open the door, but instead the King turned to the Bishop and said: "To some men, death is just the beginning. Woe to the man who dies outside the knowledge of God, and woe to the man for that he show pity to such a man as this."

𝕿he King traveled along with Bishop Jacob all the way back to Bishopscourt, but the Bishop would not speak and the King did nothing to force him. They rode slowly up the pebbled path to the main estate, tree-lined and magnificent, where the Bishop lived with his few servants. The horse master immediately took the reins and led the horses to be fed and watered. The King usually liked to admire the well-manicured grounds of which the Bishop took secular pride: the fountains, the watercourse way alive with lilies and migrating butterflies, the carved masonry and the sculpted shrubbery, but now he followed the Bishop to the main house without comment. Jacob left King Sigmus in a small parlor with a glass of strong ale while he left to change into more suitable clothes. The King watched him go, and he wondered at the man he thought that he knew. When the Bishop once again entered, he was dressed in black leggings, and blue shirt, over which he wore a grey waistcoat. The King rested comfortably on a leather sofa.

"I have ordered dinner to be served as soon as possible," Jacob said. "If you would care to rest . . ."

"No, no, Sigmus," replied. "Please sit down Jacob and let us speak like friends."

Jacob sat down on an adjacent sofa but he took nothing to drink. His face was haggard, but beautiful in the way that something loved, something cherished and unique is beautiful. The King spoke thoughtfully.

"I have known you for years, Jacob. You and I are friends and we have broken bread together. Do you now raise the dead that they may live again?"

"The Lord raised the dead child, Sigmus, not I."

"The Lord works through the saints, Jacob. Are you a saint now?"

"I am a servant, Sigmus. I have always been a servant and it is my desire only to serve the Lord. With God all things are possible. With God, all things are one."

"You frighten me, Jacob, and it is not well for that a King be frightened."

"Fear the Lord," Jacob replied tenderly. "Do not fear me my friend."

"And the devil," Jacob, "do we fear the devil as well?"

"The devil is a deceiver," said Jacob. "The devil works his evil through lies and sickness and corruption. Be frightened, but do not fear the devil, for he must be fought, engaged, and conquered with the words of Christ. The devil fears the word of the Lord more than you should fear the devil."

Later that evening the King was shown to the guest bedroom, the finest room on the estate. He sat on the edge of the bed with a candle and said a prayer before laying back. Outside the window faced the tower, *King Orry's Tower*. The King knew of the legends around the fabled tower and in truth he loved to hear such stories. Now he only gazed out the window as the clouds shifted, revealing the crescent moon and the starlit glow against the stone battlements of the tower. Crows and other night birds flew in and out of the silvery moonlight. The King lay with his eyes upon the starlit battlements and his mind turned to the prisoners interred inside the Bishop's Prison. How long he stared at the stone tower he never knew, but he soon fell asleep and was visited by a powerful and cryptic dream.

The King looked up to the top of the tower where the necromancer was chained and he secretly feared to look upon it lest he be discovered by the hated necromancer and fall beneath his terrible spell. But his fear, however, only made him more determined to go through with his plan to destroy the terrible wizard to save his people from further misery. Only the stone tower and the heavy chains and the protection of the bishop prevented the necromancer from escaping, and bishop after bishop sacrificed their own freedom to guard the terrible tower lest the necromancer bring forth beasts and monsters and giant leviathans to bring it down.

But the bishop was dead. He had been found broken and crumpled beneath the stone tower one bitter morning. No one knows if he was cast down, or if he jumped of his own volition, but the people became more convinced that the necromancer was stirring again and that he would soon escape. Strange noises now came from the tower and the people were frightened. They called for their King to save them, and now the King stood overlooking the frightening tower and his thoughts were turned to murder. He drew his sword as he burst through the door and ascended the stairs to the top of the tower. The key was hanging on a peg and he snatched it and quickly opened the door.

Inside a man was manacled to the cold stone wall and tried to stay warm with a single tattered blanket. When the prisoner saw the King, he looked at him indifferently even though he could see the rage in his eyes.

"It is your turn to die," said the King. "Prepare yourself."

"Are you upset about the bishop?" said the necromancer. "Ask it, and I shall return him to life."

"You would do better to bring yourself back to life," replied the King, and then he plunged the sword through the body of the necromancer.

As the King was descending the steps of the tower he met the bishop who had only just returned to life. The King was astonished and stood as if rooted to the spot.

"You should have taken my advice," said the necromancer through the mouth of the bishop. "Instead, I have taken your advice."

Then the necromancer took hold of the King with powerful hands and raised him above his head, smashing him on the stone steps like a broken doll.

King Sigmus woke with a shudder and sat up in bed with a jolt. Yes, it was only a dream and he was in no danger. His heart was beating wildly and his breathing came in short gasps. He stood up and went to the table near the window where a pitcher of water was set. Splashing some water in his face, he cupped his hands together and scooped the cold water and brought it to his lips. It tasted sweet. Then he opened the window and felt the rush of cold air sweep into the room.

The King stared at the tower, still infused with the faint starlight from above and still imbued with an air of unsettling eeriness from long centuries of neglect and abandonment. The dream had so unsettled him now that he needed to clear his mind before he would be able to sleep again. Without lighting a candle he sat down in the chair near the window and reflected, and this is when the devil entered his body once more and waited.

The more he thought about his dream, the more disturbed he became with the actions of Jacob. Of course he knew that Jacob was a good man, a devout man of God, but he could not shake the uneasiness that crept into his body like a numbing icy swell. And then he thought about Lucifer and how he had been cast out of heaven for his pride and his unwillingness to serve man, and he

knew that to imitate God and the ways of God was abhorrent and evil, for the
Lord had said not to suffer a witch to live. Yes, the King believed that the Lord
worked through the saints, but how did one know the difference between a
saint and . . . a sorcerer? In his confusion, he fell asleep again in the chair and
woke in the bright light of morning. Bishop Jacob was sitting in a chair
reading from the scriptures.

"Ride with me Jacob. I must go to the Bishop's Prison, for there is something I
must do and I ask you to come with me."

Jacob rose from his seat and nodded his assent. "I must speak with my
servants before I go, Sigmus. I shall meet you in a few minutes."

Soon the King, along with Bishop Jacob, was seen riding away toward
Castletown and the dreaded Bishop's Prison, but this time there was an
unaccustomed urgency on the part of the King. They waited to be ferried
across the water but already a distance had grown between the two men, each
of which was lost in private thought, and the somber empathy of the King was
balanced by the soft, ethereal splendor of the Bishop, for he was changed
forever.

Stephan, the keeper, met them on the other side and he nodded respectfully to
the King, for he recognized him. "I apologize," he said," but I am not prepared
for a visit from the King. I would have arranged something for you to eat, my
lord."

"That is unnecessary, Stephan," the King replied. "The Bishop and I will go
into the tower. See that we are not disturbed, and do not follow us."

With King Sigmus leading the way, the two men walked together up the steep,
ascending stairs with only the illumination from the key-lights to guide them.
The intensity of the King increased with each subsequent step as if he himself
were being interred, or that a weight he carried only became heavier with each
step. The Bishop saw this and prayed that the King be strong and resolute, for
he was convinced that something important was about to happen.

They did not stop to see *Kerron the Blasphemer*, they did not stop to see *Himmer
the Village Killer*, nor did they stop at any other door but instead ascended
directly to the top where Barabbas was kept. The King had a special key in his
possession which would open any door. He took it out of his pocket and then
turned to the Bishop.

"I have decided to let Barabbas go free," he announced suddenly.

Jacob looked surprised. "I thought that you said his sin is unforgivable?"

"It is," Sigmus admitted. "But tell me, Jacob, I thought that you were impressed with such signs of pity, so on this day I will show it. To some men, death is just the beginning. Woe to the man who dies outside the knowledge of God, and woe to the man for that he show pity for such a man as this."

"It is your privilege," Jacob responded. "But can he be trusted, Sigmus?"

"He can now," the King responded as he unlocked first one door and then the other.

Inside was dark but they could see a faint outline of a man laying prostrate on the floor and covered with a blanket. Sigmus spoke up.

"Go inside and rouse him, Jacob. I'm sure he will be happy to see you."

Bishop Jacob stepped inside the putrid cell and walked confidently to the dirty mass on the floor beside him. Beneath the blanket was only an oily skin of what had once been a man, now slimy and covered with crawling vermin. Suddenly he looked up with a look of amazement and turned around just as the iron door slammed shut behind him.

"Barabbas is free," the devil said through the mouth of the King. "But you will take his place, for as you know, the King dislikes sorcery of every kind."

And suddenly the Bishop knew to whom he spoke as the recognition nearly made him sick. The devil saw his condition as the shock overcame him, and his triumph was now complete.

"And so here ends the life of the righteous *Jacob, Saint of Kirk Michael*, and he began to laugh. "I hope you are not hungry," he added, "for you will have much time for fasting." Then he turned and walked away.